D1524429

L.H. COSWAY

HOW THE

Light

GETS IN

There is a crack in everything.

That's how the light gets in.

- Leonard Cohen, "Anthem"

One

"Ms. Jackson" by OutKast pumped in my ears.

I bobbed my head as I mixed a cosmo, while my co-worker, Danni, shot me a grin from the other end of the bar. The crowds pulsated on the dance floor and hands clutching crumpled bills vied for my attention.

It was just another Saturday at *FEST*, the nightclub my aunt Yvonne managed. I'd been working here for two months, ever since I moved from Dublin to New York, and I had to say, even if the work was exhausting, the tips were phenomenal. You didn't get tips like these in Ireland.

Not unless you worked at a strip club.

And I wasn't talking about mixing drinks at the bar of said strip club.

There was also an energy to this city I hadn't anticipated. It really didn't sleep. There always seemed to be something happening. Any hour of the day or night you could find a comedy gig, or an interactive theatre show, or even a doga class. That's right, yoga for dogs. Whatever floated your boat, you could find it here.

I never expected to end up in a place like this. In all honesty, I thought I'd stay in Dublin forever. Like, forever-ever. When you lived from pay check to pay check, life came with its limitations. But then Yvonne offered to set me up with a job, not to mention let me stay in her apartment. How could I say no to that?

When Gran was still alive, I would've flat-out declined, but she passed away last year. I didn't have anything to stay put for anymore, and it was an odd feeling. For so long I had an excuse not to leave, then I had none.

So I took the leap.

"What's your name, gorgeous?" a suit asked from the other side of the bar. The first few buttons of his shirt were undone, his tie loose and his grin even looser.

"Name's Evelyn, what can I get you?" I replied, professional smile in place. I wasn't a big fan of being hit on by punters, but such was life when you worked a bar. Some nights I wondered if I should take one home, let them warm my bed for a while, but I always thought better of it. I wasn't made for one-night stands. Mostly because I fell in love too easily. A charming smile and a well-placed compliment and I was handing over the keys.

During most of my twenties, my misguided, empty heart constantly looked for a person to fill it. Now I was coming to learn that the only one who could repair my heart was me. I had to find happiness within myself before I found it with someone else.

I wasn't there yet, but I was working on it.

"I love your accent. I'll take a whiskey sour, on the rocks. Don't think I've seen you here before. You new?"

I nodded as I put his drink together and did my best to be heard over the music. "Yeah, been here a couple of weeks."

"Really? Do you like New York?"

"Yeah. It's a great place to live. Expensive, but great."

"Well, if you ever need anyone to show you around, give me a call," he said and handed me a business card. I took it without even looking at the name and slipped it in my pocket to dispose of later.

"Sure. That'll be eleven dollars," I replied and handed him his drink.

He took a sip, slid me a twenty, then disappeared back into the fray of the nightclub.

"That accent of yours gets all the best tips," Danni said, an annoyed slant to her mouth.

"That's just because nobody can tell where I'm from. I'm ninety-nine per cent convinced all Americans think Irish people talk like Leprechauns."

Danni chuckled. "Don't be so xenophobic."

"You're the xenophobic ones."

"You're both goddamn xenophobic," said Ger, the third bartender on shift tonight. "Now get back to work. I'm drowning here."

I shot him an apologetic look and hustled to take more drink orders. By the time my shift was done, I was ready to keel over and expire, but again, I loved it. I loved the electricity of the city, the never-ending customers at the bar, the loud, deafening music, and the sheer exhaustion you felt at the end.

You could say positivity was my New Year's resolution. Whatever my situation in life, I was determined to make the best of it. When I was young, cheeriness was my default setting, but then life had its way with me.

After I lost Sam I could never see the sun, even when it was beaming in the sky.

Now my goal was to leave the darkness behind.

It's what he would've wanted.

I was chomping at the bit for a nice, hot shower and at least ten hours of sleep as I rode the subway to my aunt's apartment in Brooklyn. It wasn't the safest method of transportation, but since driving wasn't an option it was my only choice. Although Yvonne and I worked in Manhattan, it didn't afford us the luxury to actually live there.

Anyway, I had a bottle of pepper spray in my bag and a rape whistle in case I ran into trouble. It was almost five a.m. by the time I got home, took my long-awaited shower, and crawled into bed in my knickers and T-shirt. I didn't wake until a little after one, but I'd slept like the dead and was deliciously rested.

I could hear Beethoven playing in the living room. Yvonne must've been home, enjoying her day off. Since she was management, my aunt usually finished work around the same time I started, so we didn't cross paths too often. It was good in the sense that we both got our alone time in the apartment, because it wasn't exactly what you'd call spacious.

This also meant I hadn't seen her for a couple days. We shared the odd text message, or Post-It note stuck to the fridge, but that was it. I could smell her signature roast chicken cooking in the oven, and the scent made my mouth water.

That was the problem with working until three or four in the morning, you always ended up eating lunch for breakfast.

Needing to pee, I pulled on some shorts and wandered down the hallway toward the bathroom, stopping when I heard Yvonne had company. A deep, masculine voice replied to something she said and I frowned. It wasn't like Yvonne to have men over. In fact, she was one of those rare fish who'd always been quite happy to stay single. Her work was her lover.

She must've heard me emerge from my room because she called out, "Evelyn, are you up?"

Usually, I'd just call back that I was and go about my business, but curiosity got the better of me. Running my fingers through my sleep-knotted hair, I wandered into the living room and froze in place when I reached the threshold.

As though consciously punctuating the significance of the moment, Beethoven's Symphony No. 7 arrived at its pinnacle point. I saw a giant wave crashing into the ocean, a volcano erupting rivulets of molten lava from its lofty peak, the sharp crack of lightning in the sky, as I came face to face with a pair of dark blue eyes I hadn't seen in almost eight years.

Dylan O'Dea.

As I live and fucking *breathe*.

Actually, strike that, I wasn't breathing. The sight of him rendered my lungs incapable of normal function.

Then I remembered I was wearing the crumpled T-shirt I'd slept in and a pair of shorts that left little to the imagination. I was also sporting gorgeous bedhead. As a result, self-consciousness kicked in.

Then I remembered this was a man who'd seen me in every possible guise, from the good, to the bad, to the ugly, and I knew any level of vanity was pointless.

"Evelyn," he said, standing. He sounded so different, so mature and grown-up. The last time I saw him he was twenty-two. He'd returned to Dublin for a fleeting visit. Now he'd be thirty.

His throat bobbed as he swallowed and ran a hand through his hair. I wondered if he felt as off-kilter as I did.

"Oh Ev, we've both been so busy with work this last week I didn't even get to tell you. I bumped into Dylan the other day. What a small world it is," Yvonne said, while Dylan's gaze never left me. Those wise, astute eyes took all of me in, from the tips of my toes to the top of my head. Old memories stirred, of a time when he could own me with a look like this one.

"He has his own perfume boutique downtown now. Can you believe it?" Yvonne continued as she looked at Dylan. "You've come a long way from St Mary's Villas, that's for sure."

He owned his own perfume franchise, actually, but no way was I admitting I'd followed his career. Don't get me wrong, I'd never actually smelled any of his products. Half of it was due to fear. I didn't want to remember him, how close we'd once been, because scent had a way of plunging you into the past.

The other half was the fact that his success made me feel like a failure. I knew it was silly, especially since I was the one who told him to go fulfil his dreams all those years ago, but a part of me felt overwhelmed by all he'd achieved.

Probably because I hadn't really achieved anything myself.

"We all have," said Dylan, eyes coming back to me again. "Yvonne invited me over for lunch to catch up. I hope you don't mind."

I waved him away. "Not at all. Sorry I'm not dressed. I work nights. It's good to see you though." My words came out in a rush, and his features warmed.

"It's good to see you, too, Evelyn."

I smiled awkwardly and fiddled with the hem of my T-shirt. Heat claimed my face and chest. His attention dipped to my bare thighs for a second, then he sat back down on the couch and crossed a leg over his knee. "I can't wait to hear all about what you've been up to these days."

That was funny, because all I could think about was our past. It was a time I'd never truly moved on from. Dylan left because he had to, but also because he thought he was bad luck. He felt to blame for what happened to Sam, and I suspected he'd never gotten over that guilt.

His stare fixed on me and there was a long moment where the two of us just . . . looked at each other.

Here was a man who had once been a boy, who had once stolen my heart, who had once been my whole entire world. Now we were virtual strangers.

Sure, I'd followed his career, but it wasn't like he gave interviews or maintained a social media presence. Dylan O'Dea was far too mysterious for all that. But I had read articles and stories in the news. They weren't top stories by any means, which was why Yvonne was vaguely in the dark as to his success, but they were still there.

And like the glutton for punishment that I was, I'd sought them out, eager for any piece of insight. It was a pointless activity, of course. It wasn't like I ever planned to find him.

"Well, I'll let you two catch up while I go check on the roast," said my aunt.

Oh, Yvonne, for someone so tuned in you are completely oblivious sometimes.

She went. I turned and headed for the drinks cabinet. God knew this occasion called for one.

"What will you have?" I asked as I picked up bottles and pretended to read the labels.

"Whiskey is good," Dylan replied, and I nodded, still not facing him.

I poured his drink, plus one for myself, then turned to hand it over. His eyes travelled up my body as I approached. "The years have been good to you, Ev. You look incredible."

I arched a brow. "I look like I just stepped out of bed."

His voice went husky. "Like I said—"

"What are you even doing here?" I kept quiet so my aunt couldn't hear.

He frowned. "Yvonne invited me."

16

"You didn't have to say yes."

He gave me an *oh, come on* look. "Nobody can say no to your aunt, Ev. You know that."

He was right. Yvonne's friendly demeanour was impossible to resist, just like mine had been once upon a time. Now I was a world-weary grump with a perennial dark cloud over my head. In fact, a lot of the world-weariness was Dylan's doing. Wait, no, that was the *old* me. I was taking my positive mojo back, the one I had when I was a girl.

"No, not many people can say no to Yvonne," I agreed and went to take a seat on the armchair. I folded my legs up under me, the ones Dylan's eyes kept wandering back to, and sipped my drink.

Yikes, whiskey was *not* a good idea first thing in the morning. Or afternoon.

I set it down and eyed Dylan in his designer suit. It was a far cry from the jeans and work shirts he used to wear at St Mary's. But I guess he was a big-shot business tycoon now. He had to look the part.

"You achieved everything you always wanted," I said.

He took a sip and lifted a shoulder. "You could say that."

"Such modesty. If your eighteen-year-old self could see you now he'd be jumping for joy."

Dylan shifted his position on the sofa, his stare intense as he asked, "You think so?"

My breath caught. It wasn't so much the question, but how he said it. How he *looked* at me while he was saying it. A simmering heat worked its way up my body.

"The chicken is looking scrumdiddlyumtious," Yvonne announced, interrupting the moment.

I looked away from Dylan, frazzled by how strongly I reacted to him. We were only making casual chit-chat, and yet, his eyes alone laid me bare. I needed to get out of there. Standing, I made my way toward my bedroom.

"Can you, um, put a plate in the oven for me? I'm not feeling so well."

Yvonne frowned in concern. "Oh no, do you think it's the flu? I heard it's going around."

"I'm not sure. Maybe. It was good seeing you, Dylan, but I should really go. I don't want you to catch anything." My words were rushed.

Dylan stood, about to say something, but I left before he could. I shut myself away in my room, but I was far too restless to get back into bed. A run felt like a good idea, so I changed into a hoodie and some tracksuit pants. I wasn't normally one for exercise, but I needed to do something to expel this pent-up tension.

"Oh, Ev," said Yvonne when I re-emerged. "Are you feeling better?"

"No, but I'm gonna go for a run. See if it clears my head," I replied and glanced at Dylan very briefly. He wore a stern frown that said he knew my game. I was avoiding spending any more time with him, but what did he expect when he just showed up out of the blue like this? At least give a girl some warning.

Once I was out of the building, I felt like I could breathe again. My mind raced through memories, while my body raced through the streets of Brooklyn. I really did love it here. I never truly understood Yvonne's lifelong fascination with the city until I stepped off the plane and hopped in a yellow taxi. I adored the frenetic energy, the anonymity, the chance to be whomever I wanted, do whatever I wanted.

I paused for breath when I got as far as the Brooklyn Bridge and gazed at Manhattan's skyline. I leaned back against a railing and took a swig from my water bottle.

I can only see my dreams clearly when I look through you first.

A phantom voice echoed in my head, one from another lifetime. Dylan always said romantic things to me, stuff you'd never expect from a teenage boy. It was one of the reasons I fell for him so hard. He was an old soul, and so intelligent. He spoke in ways that set my seventeen-year-old heart aflutter.

"Hey, you got the time?" another jogger asked as he passed me by.

I pulled out my phone to check the screen. "Almost two."

"Thanks," he replied and kept going.

It was a welcome interruption, since it cut me off from wandering too deep into memories. All that would achieve was nostalgia, and nostalgia was a dangerous game when the person at the centre of it suddenly reappeared in your life.

19

I jogged to the apartment, figuring Dylan had to be gone by now. It had been over an hour since I left. When I walked inside, Yvonne was in the kitchen cleaning up.

"That was incredibly rude of you, Evelyn," she said, not making eye contact. It was something she did when she was really pissed. Her voice went all stern, but she never looked you in the eye.

"Yvonne, I haven't seen Dylan in a really long time, and the way things ended between us . . ." I ran a hand over my mussed ponytail. "How did you expect me to react?"

"I thought you'd be pleased. All that was a long time ago, Ev."

"Don't you dare undermine what happened," I said, voice tight. "You cannot even imagine—"

"Yes, I can. I was there with you, cried with you for endless nights."

I held up a hand. "Look, I'm not doing this right now. I'll talk to you later. Maybe then you'll realise I'm right."

I walked away from her and stalked into my bedroom, slamming the door behind me like a moody teen. The funny thing was, I'd never actually been a troublesome teenager. In fact, I was much easier to get along with then than I was now.

I procrastinated in my room all day: dicking around on Facebook, plucking my eyebrows, experimenting with nail polish. I didn't want to face Yvonne. I hated fighting with her, but she just didn't understand how

20

seeing Dylan again affected me, how it tossed my heart in a blender and smushed it right up.

How it made me *want* things I had no business wanting.

No business at all.

Two

Later that night, I walked into *FEST* still feeling frazzled. Once tensions simmered down between Yvonne and me, I planned to quiz her on everything she spoke about with Dylan. It was foolish, but I had to know.

It took me a minute to stash my things in the locker room and then I was at the bar, taking endless drinks orders.

"You get up to much today?" Danni asked as she mixed a margarita.

I saw the love of my life for the first time in eight years.

"Nope, not much."

"Yeah, me neither. I stayed in bed and watched a marathon of Jersey Shore."

"A highly productive day, then," I joked.

She grinned. "Oh, yah."

"Can I get a pint of lager? Whatever's best here," came a voice and an unwelcome, pleasurable shudder ran through me. *That voice.* He could read the phonebook aloud, and I'd be a captive audience of one.

"Still drinking lager?" I asked. "Some things don't change." My outward demeanour was cucumber cool, while on the inside I was flustered, too hot, like I'd bitten down on a chili pepper.

"A lot of things don't change," Dylan said as he reached up to loosen his tie. Danni mistook him for just another customer, and went to serve someone else. I studied Dylan and again, wondered why he was here.

"So, Yvonne told you where I work," I guessed as I pulled his pint. "You two must've had quite the cosy convo over lunch."

"You missed a lovely meal," Dylan replied.

"I was under the weather."

"And you go jogging when you're ill now? That's new," he went on, the left side of his mouth lifting in amusement. There was a charming lilt to his voice that drew a smile out of me.

"Yep. A good vigorous jog drives out all the pathogens," I replied and handed him his drink. "Ten dollars, please."

Dylan pulled out a flashy black credit card, and I took it without comment. "Runaway" by Kanye West came on and it was funny, because half of me wanted to run away from this whole encounter. The other half was glued to the spot, eyes wide and waiting for Dylan to reveal his intentions.

The lyrics were oddly reminiscent of our teenage years. Dylan had always been good at finding things wrong with the world. His true talent expressing what he didn't like. Maybe I should've run away from him back then, that way I might never have caught his illness. He never would've taught me to be dissatisfied with my lot.

I handed him his card and a moment of quiet passed in the loud bar.

His eyes wandered to my top. "Did Yvonne pick the uniforms here? I'll have to send her my thanks."

I shook my head at him just as a customer asked me for a rum and Coke. "No, I think that was someone higher up," I replied as I made the drink.

"Probably a man," Dylan said.

"Probably," I agreed. The uniform at *FEST* consisted of a black top with a sweetheart neckline, and tight black jeans. The male members of staff wore similarly black fitted shirts and jeans.

"So, do you ever talk to Conor and Amy these days?" I asked. They were Dylan's two closest friends when we were growing up. I used to think of the three of them as a gaggle of misfits in a place where it was safer to be just another sheep in the herd.

"Amy's living in London now. She's married with kids, working in film. And Conor's actually the COO of my company," Dylan replied, and the news surprised me. I didn't think he'd keep in touch with anyone from the old days. I knew I didn't. I certainly didn't think he'd make his old friend Chief Operating Officer of his business.

"Well, Amy always was obsessed with that little camcorder of hers. And Conor has a good head on his shoulders. To think he might've become a boring old accountant," I said.

"Conor's business sense is half the reason for *Dylan*'s success. He's the strategies, I'm the ideas."

"Right. And how are things over at *Dylan* HQ these days?" I asked.

That was the name of his perfume brand. I thought it was pretty savvy to name a women's perfume after a man they'd probably drop their knickers for in a heartbeat. At the same time, it was pretentious as fuck. Well, it would be if I didn't know Dylan so well. My guess was the name choice was somebody else's idea. Probably Conor's.

"We just opened our new store in New York and things are going well. Yvonne told you that's where she found me, right? She stumbled into the shop last week."

"Yeah, she said."

"You should come by tomorrow if you're free. I'd love to show you around."

"Perfume's not really my thing."

Dylan raised a disbelieving eyebrow. "You mean to tell me you're not gardening up a storm on some rooftop here in New York?"

I frowned, the weight of the world sinking a hole in my gut. "I don't do that anymore," I said, subdued.

Now his brows drew together in perplexity. "You don't garden?"

I huffed a breath. "What's the point? Everything you grow just ends up dying."

With that I walked to the other end of the bar and tended to some customers. Dylan remained seated, sipping on his lager while he watched me work. I found it disconcerting, especially how he brought up the whole gardening thing. You could say I was the one who first introduced Dylan to flowers, and the ways you could combine them to create pretty scents.

His signature and most popular perfume was called *E.V.* Sometimes I'd catch sight of it in a shop window and wonder if he'd named it after me, since everybody called me Ev. Then I'd think better of the foolish notion and continue on my way.

Besides, it probably stood for something pretentious and nonsensical, like *Evocative Vision* or *Eclipse Voyeur*. His other scents had names like *Synaesthesia* and *Limerence*, so it wasn't a huge stretch.

When there was a lull in customers, I pulled myself together and returned to Dylan. His glass was almost empty.

"Want another?"

"Sure."

I quietly took his old glass and replaced it with a new one. "Let's just . . . not talk about gardening. It's sort of a sore subject for me."

"No, I understand," Dylan replied. He'd obviously done some thinking over the last half hour and come to the realisation of why I no longer grew things.

I didn't know what to say, so I busied myself wiping clean the bar top.

"I used to be the pessimistic one," he said. "Feels like we switched roles."

"You've left your fatalistic ways behind?" I asked, curious.

"Guess I've realised life's not so bad."

I shot him a smirk. "Few bob in your pocket will do that."

He gave a self-deprecating smile. "Maybe."

"And what do you do nowadays in your spare time? I mean, if ranting about the injustice of the world no longer does it for you, you must have a good sixteen hours spare in the day for other stuff."

Dylan laughed, the sound like water to the desert of my heart. "Mostly, I work. I try to develop new perfumes, figure out ways to make people want to buy them. Doesn't leave a lot of room for much else."

"So," I hedged, glancing briefly at his bare ring finger. "No wife?"

He gave a faint smile, eyes wandering in the direction mine had gone. "Why, you interested?"

I rolled my eyes. "Oh, yeah. Sign me up."

"The job's yours. When can you start?"

I pursed my lips and tried not to smile, but I couldn't help it. Dylan had always been a sly flirt. You thought you were having a regular conversation and then *bam*, you were in the middle of a full-on seduction fest.

"Who's to say I don't have a husband?"

His grin was knowing. "Yvonne said you're single."

Damn my aunt and her big mouth. I narrowed my gaze at him playfully. "I have to get back to work now."

"Go ahead. I'll just sit here and enjoy myself."

"You do that."

Two hours later, Dylan was still at the bar. He alternated between watching me work and replying to texts on his phone. I wondered if it was business or personal. Probably business, since he mentioned that's all he had time for these days. And there was no wife in the picture. I couldn't help being pleased by that fact.

Although, that didn't mean there wasn't a girlfriend.

When my shift ended, I took my time balancing my till and cleaning up the bar, thinking Dylan would get bored and leave, but he didn't.

"Don't you have a bed to get to?" I asked as I buttoned up my coat.

Dylan followed me out and opened the door for me, all chivalrous. I suspected he might be after an old-time's-sake shag, but then he said, "Let me buy you breakfast."

"It's three a.m."

"And we're in New York. You can get breakfast here any time you want."

"The land of miracles," I deadpanned, but I was charmed. Very charmed. And too easily.

"Come on," he said and offered his arm. "I'm in the mood for blueberry pancakes."

I gave a sigh and linked my arm through his. "Fine, but you're buying."

"What kind of gentleman would I be if I didn't?"

"I don't know why people think being a gentleman is a good thing. When I think of the word all I see is some snobbish eighteenth-century fop in a Jane Austen novel."

"You're right. I'm more of a working-class hero."

I pointed a finger at what he was wearing. "Not in that suit."

"I have to dress this way for work," he said, seeming pleased with our banter. "If I didn't, nobody would take me seriously."

"Well, it doesn't need to be Gucci. You could don some Dunnes Finest and still look the part."

His laugh made me feel all shimmery inside, like I was a teenager all over again. "I don't think they have Dunnes Stores over here, Ev."

"A pity, they do some nice stuff. Affordable, too."

He shook his head, and we stopped in front of a small diner. "Here we are."

The place looked a little grotty, but it had a cosy charm. "Is this one of those hidden gems? Did you find it on TripAdvisor?"

"Nope. I spotted it from down the street and thought it looked decent," he replied.

"What kind of self-respecting millennial are you? You didn't even read a review first."

"Food's food, Ev. Now get your arse inside." He placed his hand to the small of my back to usher me in. It was the first time he'd touched me in years, and I had all kinds of feelings. Feelings it'd take me a bottle of wine and a quiet evening to unravel.

We got a booth, the leather worn from overuse. I sat on one side and Dylan sat on the other. He clasped his hands together and gazed at me, like he couldn't believe his luck that we were sitting across a table from one another. I picked up the menu and busied myself studying each item, a tad nervous. There was something about the one-on-one time that ramped up my anxiety. At least back at the bar I had work to focus on.

As it happened, they did serve pancakes, but I opted for some scrambled eggs on toast. Dylan told the waiter he'd have the same.

"You changed my mind," he said and closed over the menu to study me. "How long have you been living here?"

"A little over two months. Yvonne's been here years though. She probably told you. I finally decided to join her."

"What made you change your mind?"

I looked away, eyes downcast as I answered, "Gran died last Christmas. She got pneumonia after an operation, and her immune system couldn't fight it."

Immediately, Dylan reached out and took my hand. His palm felt nice, warm and dry, and I savoured the quiet moment of empathy.

"I'm sorry," he murmured. "I always liked her."

"And she liked you. The way her face used to light up when you'd come with me to visit . . . it was something else."

"I visited her on my own once," Dylan confessed and my eyes widened in surprise.

"You did?"

"Towards the end, right before I left the Villas, I needed someone to talk to," he replied. "And she always gave the best advice."

I leaned forward, interested. "What did you ask her?"

Dylan let go of my hand and sat back, his expression sincere. "I asked her how to convince you to come away with me."

My breath caught. Gran never told me Dylan went to see her. Maybe she thought it was for the best. "And what did she say?"

He exhaled and leaned forward to rest both elbows on the table. His eyes flickered between mine when he replied, "She said I needed to let you make your own decisions. That if I pushed you, we'd both only end up regretting it."

I fiddled with my napkin, smoothed my finger down its folded edge and muttered quietly, "She was a wise lady."

"That she was," Dylan agreed.

The server came with our food, and we both tucked in. I was still eating when Dylan finished, but he simply sat back, sipped his coffee and watched me.

"What?" I asked.

"You're so much older."

"Jeez, thanks."

"I didn't mean you look old. It's different. It's like you've grown into your face."

"You don't half know how to dig yourself a hole."

His expression was amiable. "Believe me, Ev. This is a compliment."

"Well, you're older, too. You're all . . . businessman-ish." *Hot businessman-ish.*

He chuckled. "Okay, that one you're gonna have to explain."

I swished my finger in the air and dabbed my mouth with a napkin. "For starters, there's the suit. Boys from the Villas only wore a suit for three reasons: wedding, funeral, court. And sometimes not even then."

"Okay, what else?"

"The way you carry yourself. It's like you know you're important. You know people depend on you. It's a world away from the Dylan I knew."

"I'm still exactly the same person, Evelyn. I just grew up. We both did."

"Hmm," I said. I was locked in his dark blue gaze when his phone lit up with a text. He'd placed it right on the table, so I saw the message flash across the screen.

Laura: You up, hon? xoxo

Well, I knew what a 'you up?' message meant when I saw one, especially when the question was followed by kisses. Dylan had been booty called, or more specifically, booty texted. Given that it was almost four in the morning, this Laura person must've been eager. Or suffering from insomnia. Or knew if she texted he'd come.

Saying that, the text didn't really surprise me. He might not have a wife, but a man as successful and handsome as Dylan had to have lady acquaintances. I bet he was fighting them off with a stick.

He quickly pressed a button and the screen went blank. He wasn't fast enough though, and he knew it.

"That was just—"

"A lady?"

His mouth twitched. "Yeah, a lady."

I gestured to his phone. "Well? Aren't you going to reply? She wants to know if you're up and you are, so . . ."

"True, but I'm busy having breakfast with an old friend."

32

"And we're just about finished, so go on, knock yourself out. Text her back."

"Ev."

"What?"

He was about to say something when he shook his head and seemed to think better of it. He slipped his phone in his pocket and stood from the table, coming around to help me out of my seat. I went to put my coat on, but he got there first. I sucked in a breath when he draped it over my shoulders and buttoned it up as I slid my arms in.

"There," he said, voice soft.

"I think I'll get a taxi home. I'm too tired for the subway."

"Come on. I'll help you hail one."

A few minutes later, I was in the back of a yellow taxi. Dylan handed the driver a few bills to pay for the journey, which I thought was kind of him. He leaned down to the window to talk to me before the driver pulled away.

"So, I'll see you tomorrow at twelve, yeah?"

I furrowed my brow. "What's tomorrow?"

"You're coming to see my shop," he said and then he was too far away for me to respond. The taxi joined traffic, and I flopped back into the seat, emitting a long breath.

A couple of days ago I would've sworn we'd never cross paths again, but I'd just had breakfast at three in the morning with Dylan O'Dea and tomorrow he wanted me to visit his perfume shop.

The most surprising thing though? I actually wanted to go. After so many years following his career from afar, I wanted to see what his life was like up close. So yeah, even though I knew it was probably a terrible idea, I was going to take Dylan up on his invite.

I was going to see what all the fuss was about.

Three

Dylan was on Sixth Avenue.

The shopfront consisted of a large, floor-to-ceiling window, framed by what appeared to be black marble. It gave a sleek and expensive impression, just like the perfumes contained within. I stood outside in my five-year-old jeans, navy parka, and scuffed Doc Martens, wondering what on earth I was doing there.

This place wasn't for me. Like I told Dylan years ago, I was more of a *Body Shop* girl. Inside, smartly dressed men and women made the rounds, chatting to customers and making suggestions on different products.

The street was noisy, a cacophony of traffic and people. I sucked in a deep breath and walked inside. Immediately, a smiling redhead greeted me. Her hair was in a neat chignon, and she wore a smart black pencil dress and pearls. I expected her to look down on me, maybe ask me to leave with that smile still on her face, but she didn't.

"Hello, and welcome to *Dylan*. Is there anything in particular I can help you with today?"

"Oh, I'm just looking," I said, hoping she'd leave me alone. I wasn't quite ready to see Dylan yet, still gathering my nerve. Last night, I'd tossed and turned, replaying the day's events in my head, trying to pick out what he wanted from me. Friendship? *Romance?*

I wished people would be up front with their intentions. Tell you straight what they were after.

"Of course, please take your time. And if you need my help I'll be right here," she said and I stepped by her.

I paused in front of a collection of perfumes in red-, pink- and purple-tinted bottles. This was Dylan's new line. I hesitated in front of the display, my throat clogged with indecision. Never before had I opened a bottle of *Dylan* perfume and taken a sniff. Not even once. Every time I considered it my entire body tensed up with anxiety, my heart thrummed and my brain scrambled.

I knew that each scent would remind me of him. Dylan was the sort of person who put his entire self into every endeavour. I'd smell the top notes and see his smile, the middle notes and remember his voice. But most of all, hidden like a secret in the bottom notes, I'd *feel* his touch.

And afterward, I'd look at my life and know there was something missing. Something vital. Like a heart that didn't beat, or an instrument that made no sound.

I'd much rather live in blissful ignorance than sink into that bottomless hole.

But standing here, with those bottles laid out in front of me, the temptation was hard to resist. Maybe the drug called Memory would be worth the comedown named Emptiness.

Feeling brave, I picked up a bottle, pulled off the cap and sprayed some on the inside of my wrist. A pair of warm, firm hands came to rest on my shoulders. I closed my eyes for the briefest second, then opened them and turned to face him. Even before I looked, I knew it was him.

He glanced from me to the bottle I held, his left eyebrow rising the tiniest bit. His voice was low, hushed, when he asked, "Do you like it?"

My mouth ran dry. "I haven't had the chance to smell it yet."

His lips curved ever so slightly as he gestured with his hand. "Then, by all means, go ahead."

Self-consciously, I placed the bottle down and brought my wrist to my nose. The line consisted of three scents; *Dylan: Rose*, *Dylan: Lily*, and *Dylan: Wildflower*.

Wildflower was the one I chose, and when I inhaled I briefly closed my eyes, because I was swept away to an alpine meadow in France. There was a sharp, clean edge to the flowery scent that made me picture snowy mountains and pale blue skies.

Dylan's gaze flickered to my wrist, focusing for a second. Then, carefully, he circled it with his fingers and lifted it to his own nose. His eyes held mine as he inhaled deeply, then gently let it drop. "That's the one I would've picked for you, too," he said, voice soft.

"It's beautiful," I replied, unable to withhold the compliment.

"You think so?" he asked, pleased.

"Yes, but I wouldn't buy it."

He started to frown. "No?"

I gestured to the price tag. "It costs one hundred dollars, Dylan. I'm pretty sure I could cobble something similar together if I really wanted to, and it'd cost me ten dollars tops."

I was talking utter crap, of course. I may have been able to make something similar, but it wouldn't have that special quality only Dylan could create. I didn't have the talent to find that one ingredient that melded all the others together, elevating them from the ordinary to extraordinary.

As they called it in the biz, Dylan was a *nose*. And a very fine and skilled nose at that.

His frown turned into a grin. "Yes, well, don't go telling that to my customers."

"You really have embraced the ways of capitalism."

"I told you it was the only way to make money."

"Yeah," I replied, remembering. "You did, didn't you?"

We stayed locked in a moment when a sweet voice interrupted. "Mr O'Dea, there's a call for you in the office."

It was the redhead from before, but she wasn't smiling like she was earlier. Instead her expression was painfully blank.

"Ah, thank you, Laura. I'll go get it now."

Laura.

His text from last night. I glanced at her name tag. She was the assistant manager.

Wow, Dylan was shagging his employees.

Though I couldn't really blame him. Laura had that whole Jessica Chastain thing going on. I wasn't above admitting that if I was the boss and some Chris

Hemsworth lookalike was working for me, I'd be taking advantage of my position of power left, right, and centre.

Or was that above, below, and from behind?

I smirked to myself and Dylan gave me a funny look, raising an eyebrow. "Inside joke," I told him, and he only raised his brow higher.

Laura cleared her throat and Dylan glanced back at her, distracted. "Is there anything else?"

"No, Mr O'Dea. Nothing else," she chirped with bite. Her tone said everything her words didn't. *Who's the blonde?*

"Come on, Evelyn. Your tour can start with my office." He took my hand and led me away from the storefront. Laura's expression gave the faintest hint of shock, but I couldn't tell if she recognised my name, or if it was because he was holding my hand.

Troublingly, touching Dylan felt as natural as ever, like there weren't years of distance between us.

His office was a lot less swanky than I expected. In fact, it was a mess. There were files and papers all over the desk. Haphazard piles of perfume samples lay in one corner, while what looked to be a mini chemistry lab was set up on a table in the other.

I pointed to it. "Does that coincide with health and safety regulations?"

He ran a hand through his hair as he went to pick up the phone. "Maybe."

"Huh," I said as I inspected the trappings.

There was some sort of oil in one beaker, and a clear liquid in another. On a chopping board was a bunch of cut-up chocolate cosmos, which was an incredibly rare flower. Eleven years ago, it would've galled me to see it like that. I picked up a piece and gave it a quick sniff. Hmm, vanilla. They were notoriously hard to grow, and I'd never tried myself. Dylan was obviously endeavouring to use them in one of his perfumes.

Then there was a glass jar full of wet, crushed wood chippings. I picked it up and gave it a sniff, too. Dylan, who had been quietly talking on the phone in the background, finally hung up. He clasped his hands together as he considered me.

"Smells like a rainy day, right?"

"I thought it was just wet wood, but now that you mention it . . ." I gave the jar another sniff and realised he was right. It smelled like going outside after a heavy shower, when the earth was at its most fragrant.

"Is this your something odd?" I asked and set the jar back down.

He shot me a questioning look.

"You once told me that there's something odd in every beautiful scent," I explained, a little shy to reveal my memory of his words so clearly. I looked down, self-conscious. "You combine something pretty with something unpleasant and the result is . . . perfection."

His eyes shimmered, and for a second I thought he might be the tiniest bit homesick. "I did have some grandiose ideas back then, didn't I?"

"It was true, though. You might've talked a lot, but you talked a lot of sense."

"You give me too much credit."

He stood and walked towards me. When he was near, my skin prickled. He reached out and my breath caught. I thought he was going to touch me, but then he picked up one of the flower petals from the chopping board. Next, he plucked some of the crushed wood from the jar and clasped both between his palms. He rubbed them together, then opened his hands and held them out to me.

"Smell," he urged.

I took a whiff and was surprised by the pleasant aroma. Dylan had mixed sweet with earthy, a combination I wouldn't normally find appealing, but somehow it worked.

"That's actually really good," I said, inhaling a second time.

He swept the petals and wood back onto the table and cleaned his hands with a cloth. "It's a work in progress. It needs something else, but it hasn't come to me yet."

"How about cinnamon?" I teased. "It'd sell well during the holiday season."

Dylan smirked. "I know you're taking the piss, but that's actually not a bad idea."

"In that case, I want ten per cent."

He chuckled. "I'll give you eight."

"Five," I countered, feeling silly. "Hold on. I'm doing it wrong."

"You're a goof," Dylan said. "Come. I want to show you the rest of the shop."

It was impressive, especially considering how competitive the location was. Dylan ended our tour on the top floor, where his products were stored and staff took inventory of stock. I wandered through the aisles, reading all the labels when I came to a small, circular-shaped window that looked onto the busy shopping street. It was old, probably original to the building, and I loved it.

I was a sucker for unconventionally shaped windows, especially circular ones. There was something mysterious about them. I glanced down towards the street and Dylan came to stand next me. We weren't touching, but his closeness alone was tactile. He'd always been like that, so much larger than life. His presence left its fingerprints all over your body.

"So, what do you think?" he asked, and though I wasn't looking, I could sense him studying my profile.

"Impressive, but there's still a few things I'd change."

"Oh?" he asked, intrigued.

I glanced at him. "You seriously care what I think?"

His expression was fond. "I always have."

I blew out a breath and looked around. "Well, for a start I'd ditch the whole 'meet and greet' at the door. It feels too much like a hard sell, and personally, I find that intimidating. I want to at least have a look around before there's a sales clerk in my face. Oh, and also, the uniforms."

"The uniforms?"

"Those plain black pencil dresses are way too stuffy. Your perfume might be elegant, but your brand is young and fresh. The staff should dress smart, but I think you should let them personalise what they do wear. All the guys and girls on your shop floor are like clones."

"Go on, Ev. Tell me how you really feel," Dylan teased, and I flushed a little.

"You asked."

"Yes, I did. And thank you. I'll take your recommendations under advisement."

I nodded at him, pleased, and turned to gaze back out the window.

He stared at me for a second, like he was thinking of something.

"What?" I asked, curious.

"Can I take you somewhere?"

"Depends on where."

"I don't want to tell you until we get there."

"Why?"

"Because if I do, you won't come."

My expression turned guarded. "In that case, no, you can't take me anywhere."

"Oh, come on, Ev. Live a little."

"I'm living just fine right here."

"You'll love this, I promise. You'll hate me at first, but then you'll love it."

Hmm, how could I say no to that? It wasn't like I had anywhere else to be. My shift at *FEST* didn't start until eight.

Dylan held his hand out to me, and deciding to take a chance—much like I did eleven years ago—I placed mine in his.

Four

Dylan took me to a farm.

We left his shop and hopped in a taxi. He rattled off an address to the driver, but given I wasn't a New York native, I still had no idea where we were going. Turned out it was a rooftop farm called Eagle Street, and it was the sort of place I would've given an arm and a leg to work at when a teenager. My old rooftop allotment had nothing on this place.

There was a stall selling produce, but Dylan convinced the owner to let us look around out back. There were rows of cabbages, beets, potatoes, onions . . . you name it. It was admittedly a remarkable place, but not really my thing. Even when I had my allotment, I mostly grew flowers and herbs. Stuff that smelled nice and looked pretty. I noticed some wildflowers growing on the edge of the farm, but otherwise it was all vegetables.

"This is the sort of place I always imagined you ending up," Dylan said.

I glanced at him as we walked. "Sometimes life doesn't turn out how you expect."

"No, it doesn't," he replied, subdued. "Still, I think you should ask the owner if there are any jobs going. Surely, you'd prefer to work here than at the bar."

"I told you, I don't grow things anymore."

He seemed unhappy with this. "Haven't you considered starting over?"

I shook my head and swallowed tightly. "No. After Yvonne left, I managed to get a transfer to one of the ground-floor flats. Gran moved in with me, and I took care of her until she passed. It was a full-time job, so I didn't have time for the allotment. Mrs O'Flaherty took over."

"That old shrew is still alive?" Dylan asked, surprised.

"Yep. She'll outlive the lot of us. All that gardening keeps her young."

Dylan smiled, looking out across the water to the city. You could see half of Manhattan from here. Not exactly what you'd expect from a farm, so it was certainly unique.

"Did you ever have time for a boyfriend when you were caring for your gran?" he asked. The question took me off guard, especially how he looked like he'd wanted to ask it for a while.

I swallowed, clasped my hands together, then nodded. "There were one or two."

"Anyone I know?"

I shot him a look. "Let's not do this, Dylan."

"What? I'm curious."

"Laura seems nice," I said, playing him at his own game.

His lips twitched, and he turned his gaze to the scenery. "Fair enough."

"So, how does that work? Do your other employees know, or is it a strictly private arrangement?" She called him *hon* and texted in the middle of the night as if she knew he'd be available. They must've at least been close, even if they weren't an actual couple.

"Laura and I shared a few nights together when I first opened the store. Obviously, not an ideal move."

"Why? She's gorgeous."

"Just because someone's gorgeous doesn't mean they'll make a good partner," he said, and I guessed he was right. Dylan had been the most attractive boy I'd ever met, but that still didn't stop our relationship from falling apart.

"I agree," I replied. "Chemistry counts for a lot though, and attraction often creates it."

His eyes warmed and I turned away, looking for a distraction. I wanted to enjoy being here. I didn't want to talk about either of our love lives.

"Can we go visit the market stall?" I asked.

"Of course," he replied and gestured with his hands. "Lead the way."

We quietly walked through the rows of produce, thoughts churning up a storm in my head. What strange, otherworldly force caused Yvonne to walk into Dylan's shop when she did? You could live in this city your entire life if you wanted and still never meet the same person twice. But I was here only two months and somehow Dylan and I found our way back to one another. It felt serendipitous.

"So, are you living in New York permanently now, or are you only here until the store gets on its feet?"

Dylan exhaled a small breath. "Honestly? It's been hard to settle anywhere. I've been moving from place to place setting up stores, but my favourite city has been

San Francisco. That's actually where I opened my first shop."

"Do you go back much?"

"Not as often as I'd like, but I have an excellent manager. He keeps things ticking over."

"And what about New York? Do you like it here?"

Dylan took a moment to consider his answer, his expression soft when he replied, "It's definitely growing on me."

My cheeks heated, and I paused to admire the marigolds for sale next to the vegetable stall. I took a second to inhale, memories flooding me. These flowers had been Gran's favourite.

"It's so odd how the scent of marigolds always takes me back to Gran," I said, marvelling. Dylan came to stand next to me, and dipped his head to smell them, too.

"There's a scientific explanation, if you care to hear it."

"You always did have an answer for everything," I teased and nudged him with my elbow.

He inhaled again, as though to demonstrate. "When we breathe in, the olfactory nerve in our brain is stimulated, which is located close to the amygdala." He paused to tap the side of my forehead. "The amygdala is a group of nuclei located in the temporal lobe of your brain, and it has an important role in your emotional reactions. Also located in the temporal lobe is the hippocampus, which helps to consolidate short- and long-term memory. So, when our olfactory nerve is given a scent, our brain is quickly connecting it to the memory it provokes, but also to the emotion associated with that memory."

"Wow," I breathed, unable to hide my fascination. Dylan was still full of interesting and unusual information, just like he'd been when he was younger.

"It's a survival mechanism we developed through evolution. If we smell smoke, we know to be on alert for a fire. If we don't smell smoke, we know everything is okay. Scent causes countless nerve signals to be set off in our brains."

"All happening in the blink of an eye," I added fondly. Dylan never failed to bring out my affectionate side, especially when he went all scientist on me.

"There are just as many molecules in a single breath as there are stars in all the galaxies. The scent from a single spray of perfume is a much grander experience when you think about it that way," he went on.

He really had a talent for making this shit sound romantic. "Where did you learn all this?" I was so curious, because there was a confidence in his knowledge now that seemed very sophisticated.

"I studied olfactory science in Los Angeles," he said. "I learned a lot of the theory behind the things I already had a talent for."

So that was it. When we learn from someone talking passionately, rather than from words on a page, it creates knowledge that feels more alive.

"Los Angeles, San Francisco, New York, you've really gotten around," I replied, impressed.

"It cost an arm and a leg to study there, but I managed to get a loan. A bit of a dodgy one, but still a loan. Thankfully, I was able to pay it back once the company took off. Conor had his MA in business by then, so he came over to help me with that side of things. And now, well, here we are."

"Your determination to succeed paid off," I said as I lifted a bunch of marigolds from the display and handed the girl some money. Dylan appeared pleased.

I shot him a side-eye. "Don't read anything into it. It's just my amygdala making me sentimental."

"I'm going to get you gardening again," he replied. "Just watch."

"It'll be a wasted effort," I told him, but the fact that he cared so much made my heart skip a beat. Dylan selected a bag of tomatoes, an onion, and some garlic. After he paid for them, he carried the plastic bag with one hand and offered the other one to me. I stared at it for a second.

"I don't have warts, Ev."

"I know that, it's just, there's no need—"

"I want to make you lunch at my house."

"Why your house?" I asked, suspicious. "I saw a deli down the street."

"My place is way better than a deli. Besides, I want to catch up some more," he said, all innocence. I still couldn't be sure if I believed him. Was the purpose of this outing to reminisce about the old days, or was he looking for more than that? *And if so, why?*

Emotionally speaking, I wasn't ready for more. And certainly not with him. Yes, my last boyfriend,

Rick, had been over a year ago, but the break-up had been messy, the relationship toxic from the start. Gran's health had started to deteriorate. I was lonely and depressed and picked the worst possible man to make me feel better.

"Okay," I finally allowed. "But I don't need to hold your hand."

He dropped his outstretched palm, his smile slipping a little. "All right, no hand-holding. Come on; let's try to find a taxi. I make the best bruschetta in all of New York."

"Bruschetta, huh? Somebody's moved up in the world." He even pronounced it correctly. "I remember the days when we used to eat frozen pizza and think it was fancy."

"Well, I've matured in many ways," he said, flirtatiously. I shot him a wry look as I threw my hand out for an oncoming taxi.

Dylan was renting an old townhouse in the East Village, which wasn't what I expected at all. With his designer suits and perfume franchise, I thought he'd be somewhere on the Upper East Side with a view of the park and lots of floor-to-ceiling windows. Instead he lived in a three-storey period house that somehow managed to feel cosy. The building was old, obviously, with vines crawling up the aged brickwork. On the inside, the original features were well preserved. It had been a while since I'd been anywhere that still had a fireplace.

"Well, what do you think?" Dylan asked as he dropped his keys in a bowl on the mantelpiece.

"I like it, feels homey," I said and followed him into the kitchen.

"The woman who owns the building, Marguerite, furnished the place," he said as I slid onto a stool by the counter and nodded.

"Definitely has that feminine touch."

"I think that's what I like about it." Dylan started to unpack the food. "Women have this way of turning houses into homes." He paused, looking thoughtful, then added, "It's all in the small details."

I murmured my agreement and watched while he prepared our lunch. He rolled up his sleeves and washed his hands, then washed and chopped the tomatoes. He tossed them in a bowl with some garlic and basil. The way he moved was effortless, like he'd practiced the recipe so many times he didn't have to think about it anymore. Next, he sliced a lemon and squeezed one half over the bowl.

"I use lemon instead of vinegar," he said, and I smiled.

"An artistic flourish?"

"Something like that." He grinned and mixed everything with his hands. He leaned down and inhaled. "One day I'll make a perfume inspired by this recipe. Here, smell," he said and held his hands out to me.

I stared at them for a second, hesitating, then leaned down to inhale. "Um, it's nice and all, but I'm not sure there's a market for bruschetta perfume, especially with all that garlic."

Dylan chuckled, a rich, hearty sound. I rolled my eyes, because what I said wasn't *that* funny. I also needed to distract myself from how his laughter created a yearning ache inside me. There was something about the masculine shape of his hands and the way his shirtsleeves were rolled up to his elbows that I found overwhelmingly attractive.

I felt a sudden, bizarre urge to lick the tomato juice from his fingers. I saw myself do it in my head, all sultry, like in the movies, where the character blinks in relief to know it was just their imagination.

"I said a perfume *inspired* by the recipe. The final product would be something entirely different," Dylan explained. "It's the sharp, tangy kick of tomato and lemon, the hint of peppery basil. I need to find a way to capture that in a wearable scent."

"Hmm," I said, not convinced. "I'll believe it when I smell it."

Dylan laughed again, eyes sparkling with merriment as he stared at me for a long moment. So long I became self-conscious.

"What?" I asked, tucking some hair behind my ear.

He shrugged. "It just feels surreal to have you here."

I pursed my lips. "Surreal good or surreal bad?"

He was quick to answer. "Good. Definitely good."

Over an hour later, I sat on Dylan's couch, belly full of bruschetta and ready for a nap. What was it about overeating that made me so sleepy?

Dylan sat on the other side of the couch, a good, safe distance between us. He rested one arm over the back of it, studying me with quiet speculation.

"Tell me about your last relationship," he said.

I scoffed. "You sound like a bad psychotherapist."

He shifted his body closer. "I can't help it. I want to know who you've been with since me."

I arched a brow. "Why?"

"Because I've got a masochistic side, so indulge it."

I blew out a breath. Over the course of the last few years, I'd made one or two unwise romantic decisions. My heart yearned to find its match, but no one ever seemed to live up to the man currently sitting across from me. Now I wondered if maybe it wasn't yearning for its match, but rather yearning for the one it lost. Dylan had been a hard act to follow, that was for sure.

"Well, my first boyfriend after you was Jonathan Miller," I said, deciding to start with the good and work my way up to the bad.

Dylan blinked. "With the braces?"

"He had them out by the time we got together," I defended. "And he was really nice, actually. Probably the nicest person I've ever been with." A lot nicer than the ones that came after him, anyway.

"I wasn't nice?" he feigned offence.

"No, nice isn't how I'd describe you. Idiosyncratic is a better word."

"Peculiar then."

"You were when compared with ninety-nine per cent of the other boys at the Villas."

"Maybe," he allowed. "So, what was it like with old Johnny Miller?"

I reached over to the coffee table to pick up my glass of wine. Before we ate, Dylan broke out an expensive bottle of white, and yes, I might've had a shift in several hours, but I couldn't say no to a glass. In the back of my mind, I wondered if he was trying to get me tipsy so I'd loosen up. Then again, he'd never needed alcohol for that. One look and he'd owned me.

I took a sip and placed it on the table. "It was . . . pleasant. He bought me gifts every month on payday. The problem was, I was always so busy with Gran, and he resented the fact that he came second. He was the one to break it off."

"Dumped by Johnny "braceface" Miller," Dylan teased. I swiped him on the arm.

"Shut up. I was heartbroken. I thought we were going to buy a bungalow together and have babies, one boy and one girl. Instead, he ended up marrying Sheena Davies."

"He went from you to Sheena?" Dylan asked, clearly perplexed.

"I guess she gave him more attention than I did, but she's so bossy. I sometimes saw them doing groceries together and she had him completely under her thumb. I actually felt a little sorry for him."

"Well, he made his choice. Any man who dumps you is an idiot in my opinion," Dylan said sincerely.

I lifted my glass, smiling as I joked, "My sentiments exactly."

"And after Jonathan?" he went on with interest.

I grimaced. *Now for the bad.* "After Jonathan, I was single for a couple of years until I met Rick." I paused, not exactly excited to get into the topic of my most recent ex. And yes, I'd had a few short flings here and there, all of them ending in heartbreak, but it wasn't necessary to tell Dylan about those.

"Do I know him?"

I shook my head. "He was from the south side, really posh, but also kind of a dick."

"Rick the dick." Dylan nodded. "Got it."

I chuckled. "That about sums him up. I was in a bad place. Gran was getting sicker and sicker, and I just needed someone to comfort me."

Dylan frowned, his brows furrowing, like he didn't enjoy the idea of me being lonely. "What happened?" he asked gently.

I exhaled. "I didn't know it at the time, but I was basically his secret bit on the side. The working-class girl he'd never dream of bringing home to his parents. I was with him for almost a year when I found out he was engaged to some girl from his hometown. His family and hers were close, so they approved of the marriage. He said he got with me because he felt trapped, but I saw him for what he was: a dirty cheat who wanted the best of both worlds."

"And you broke up with him then?" Dylan asked, jaw firm. He looked angry.

I nodded. "Yes, but . . ."

"But what?"

"He wasn't too keen on letting me go. He kept showing up at the flat, and I was too weak to tell him no, so . . . I let him stay the night. That happened a few times. He kept telling me he was going to break off the engagement, but I soon figured out he never would.

That's when I finally pulled together the strength to end it for good."

"Ev." Dylan frowned, reaching out to clasp my shoulder. "I hate that you went through that."

I shrugged, trying to keep a straight face and not get all mushy and emotional. "You live, you learn."

His hand moved from my shoulder to tuck a fallen strand of hair behind my ear. I sucked in a quick breath at his touch.

"I should've come back for you," he murmured.

"You did."

"I should've tried harder to convince you to come with me."

"I only would've told you the same thing I told you the first time. I would've told you to go fulfil your dreams."

"I think your exact words were, *if you ever come back here I'll never talk to you again*," he said, the edges of his lips curving.

"Oh, the irony," I said with a quiet laugh.

He was fiddling with my hair now, his gaze transfixed by what his fingers were doing. "Teenagers, so melodramatic," he went on, voice soft. His hand moved down along my neck and goosebumps rose where he touched me. He made a low hum in the back of his throat, like touching me relaxed him, and I closed my eyes for a second.

"You've always been so incredibly beautiful, Ev," he whispered.

I opened my eyes and got lost in his. The deep, dark blue of his irises was a seductive prison I could happily reside in. His hand gripped my shoulder, and I snapped to my senses. I pushed off the couch and went to grab my coat and handbag while checking my phone.

"Is that the time? I have to get going."

"Ev, wait a second."

I turned back to him, but closed my eyes for willpower. If I looked at him, I might do something incredibly silly, like jump onto his lap and kiss him. I was twenty-nine years old. I couldn't be kissing Dylan O'Dea.

Because when I did, I was his. Completely, utterly his.

"What?" I whispered.

"I'm sorry if I was too forward. I shouldn't have touched you like that."

I shook my head. "You don't need to apologise." Because he might've been the one to touch me, but I knew my eyes encouraged him.

"Still, I hope I didn't offend you."

"You didn't, I promise. I'll see you around, Dylan."

With that I turned and walked out into the hallway and to the door. It opened just as I reached it and in walked Conor. I paused mid-stride, surprised. Not because this was the first time I'd seen him in years, but because he'd undergone quite the transformation. Gone were the glasses and scruffy Afro. They'd been replaced with a tightly shaved haircut, a suit and, I imagined, some serious laser eye surgery.

Conor had shed his awkward eighteen-year-old skin to become one seriously hot piece of arse. If I wasn't still reeling from Dylan's re-entry into my life—had I not known Dylan was here *in* New York—I might have actually asked Conor out on a date.

"Conor, wow," I breathed.

"Evelyn, my God." He looked frazzled, like he'd had a busy day and seeing me threw him for a loop. Wait, had Dylan not told him about running into Yvonne?

"Hey, it's great to see you."

"Yes, you, too. Man, it's been a long time."

"The years have been good to you. Really good," I said, and he smiled at the compliment. The old Conor might've gone shy and flushed, but not this Conor. *This* Conor took it with all the suave sophistication of a successful COO.

"I could say the same for you. You look gorgeous."

Dylan came to stand next to me, emitting a barely perceptible grunt of irritation. Conor ran a hand over his head. He had a really nicely shaped skull, now I could actually see it. His gaze flickered back and forth between Dylan and me, trying to read the room.

"So, uh, how did you end up in New York?" he asked, focusing back on me.

"I've only been here a short while. I moved over to join Yvonne. She's been here a couple of years, actually—"

"Yvonne?" Conor's eyes lit up like it was Christmas.

I chuckled. "Yes, Yvonne." I'd almost forgotten about his old crush.

"She's in town?"

"Yep. She manages the bar I work at. It's called *FEST*."

He blew out a breath. "I've literally walked by that place a hundred times."

"Well, it's a small world, you know. Yvonne walked into *Dylan* last week, and that's how we reconnected," I said, gesturing between Dylan and me. "So, you two are living together?"

Conor nodded, smiling. "We didn't think there was much point renting two separate places, so we're roommates. Hey, do you know what? We should all go out for dinner sometime. Have a catch up. You, me, Yvonne and Dylan."

I just about caught Dylan's smirk. "Still jonesing for the aunt, huh?"

Conor cast him a look. "It's been a long time. It'd be nice to get together."

"Yeah, it would. Um, let me ask Yvonne and get back to you. Right now, I've got to get going though, but we'll talk soon."

"Yeah, talk soon," Conor agreed, and I slipped out the door. I didn't look at Dylan. I needed to leave. I needed some time to clear my head.

I needed to absorb the fact that I still wanted him. After all these years . . . it made me feel like a teenager all over again. But more than that, it made me feel excited, because when I'd been Dylan's, he'd made me his world.

And like all humans, I craved being everything to someone.

Five

When I arrived home, I took a long, cold shower.

Okay, so maybe it wasn't *that* cold, but it was definitely long. I needed time under the water to clear my head. Dylan's touch popped and fizzled in my brain, causing all sorts of girlish, fluttery reactions.

I stepped out of the bathroom with one towel around my body and another wrapped around my hair. Yvonne stood in her bedroom doorway, having just finished a phone call.

"Well, don't you look spic and span," she commented, our previous spat all but forgotten. That was the way of things with us. Last night's argument was yesterday's news. We'd moved on.

"I've got work in an hour," I replied. "Oh, also, guess who I saw today?"

"Was it Chris Kristofferson?"

I frowned. "No."

She gave a shrug. "I just like saying the same Chris Kristofferson. Rolls off the tongue."

"Well, it wasn't him. It was Conor Abrahams. Remember? From the Villas?"

"You mean the kid you used to pal around with who tried to kiss me once?" she asked wryly and followed me into my bedroom.

"Yes, that's the one," I replied, choosing to leave out the fact that he wasn't a kid anymore. I wanted to witness Yvonne's reaction when she saw him in person. His transformation would stun her. "He actually helps run Dylan's company now. They invited us out to dinner some night when we're all free. What do you think?"

She smiled. "Oh really? That's sweet of them. Sure, I'm game for it."

"Great, I'll let them know."

Yvonne took a seat on my bed while I changed into my work uniform. I had no embarrassment about stripping down in front of my aunt. We didn't roll that way.

"So," she hedged. "I guess Dylan managed to catch you at the bar? He mentioned he might pay you a visit."

I nodded. "Yeah, he stopped by."

"And?"

"And nothing. We chatted about old times. It was nice."

"Ev, your childhood sweetheart is some sort of perfume business mogul, not to mention he's even more handsome than he was as a boy. Surely, it was more than nice."

"I enjoyed spending time with him, Yvonne, but I'm not interested in starting something romantic," I replied. That big, fat lie sat heavy on my tongue.

"Oh," she said. "Well, that's disappointing."

"Why? Were you hoping for a big splashy wedding or something?"

"Don't be like that. You two had something special, but you never really got a chance to see where it might go. It's not anyone's fault that—"

"Look, I'm late for work," I said. "And I need to get ready, so . . ."

Yvonne glanced at me sadly and nodded. "Of course. I'll see you in the morning."

***

Dylan left his business card with Yvonne, which was convenient because I didn't have his phone number. What wasn't convenient was the fact that it only had his office number, not his personal line. It also had an email, so I tried that instead. I didn't want to call his office and get through to the delightfully hostile Laura.

Tuesday 09:43 evflynn21@gmail.com to dylanod@dylanscents.com

Well, this is awkward. We forgot to exchange numbers. Yvonne had your business card, so I thought I'd try you on the old email instead. We're free for dinner tomorrow night if you and Conor are up for it.

Let me know.

Ev.

I read the email back several times, thinking it sounded stilted, but unable to come up with a better way to phrase the message. Deciding to hell with it, I hit send. I doubted he checked this email very often anyway. If he wanted to have dinner, he knew where to find me.

To my surprise, my email pinged with a response ten minutes later. I was lying in bed, still in my PJs, when I opened it up.

Tuesday 09:54 dylanod@dylanscents.com to evflynn21@gmail.com

Tomorrow night is perfect. We'll pick you and Yvonne up at your place around eight.

63

Love,
Dylan.

I couldn't help smiling at how he signed off. I enjoyed his affection, even if I was wary of returning it. I typed out a reply.

Tuesday 09:56 evflynn21@gmail.com *to dylanod@dylanscents.com*

Eight is good. Dress code?

Tuesday 09:57 dylanod@dylanscents.com *to evflynn21@gmail.com*

Anything. You always look beautiful.

I bit my lip and closed my eyes. Man, he was charming.

Tuesday 09:59 evflynn21@gmail.com *to dylanod@dylanscents.com*

Seriously. I need to know. I felt so underdressed at your store.

It was true. I'd had a Julia Roberts *Pretty Woman* moment stepping inside that place. I didn't want to feel that way again, especially if Dylan decided to take us to some swanky Michelin-star restaurant where men had to wear a tie to get in.

Tuesday 10:02 dylanod@dylanscents.com *to evflynn21@gmail.com*

Underdressed sounds interesting . . .

Tuesday 10:03 evflynn21@gmail.com *to dylanod@dylanscents.com*

That's it. I'm not coming.

Tuesday 10:04 dylanod@dylanscents.com *to evflynn21@gmail.com*

That would be a travesty ;-)

Tuesday 10:07 evflynn21@gmail.com to dylanod@dylanscents.com

Ugh, you're irritating in emails. Do you know that? If I wear the wrong thing, on your head be it. See you tomorrow.

P.S. This is my number if you need to get in touch: 415 561 5670

Tuesday 10:08 dylanod@dylanscents.com to evflynn21@gmail.com

Thanks! See you tomorrow. xxx

I thought that was the end to our conversation, but several minutes later my phone lit up with a call from a number I didn't recognise.

"Hello?"

"If we're exchanging numbers, this is mine," came Dylan's voice. I liked how the husky quality of it sounded on my phone.

"Right. Thanks," I replied, then paused a moment. "You could've just emailed me."

"Emails are too easy to hack."

"Oh, is your number that valuable? Is your first name Beyoncé?"

"No. I'm just security aware." He let out a sexy exhalation. "Sassypants."

I chuckled, mostly because I couldn't think of anything to say, and there was another pause, a long one.

Dylan exhaled again. This time it sounded strained. "Evelyn . . ."

"Yes?" I replied, eager.

"I want to . . . date you."

"You do?" I squeaked, then cleared my throat. "I mean, do you?"

"I want to get to know you again, if you'll let me."

He wanted to date me? The very idea put a big, silly smile on my face. But then, I frowned. Would it be selfish to get into a relationship with Dylan when I was still finding my feet after losing Gran? I'd made a resolution to try to be happy, but I knew I wasn't there yet. And over the years, I always thought I needed someone else to be content, always tried to find myself in other people. If I got into a relationship with Dylan now, would I be repeating the same mistakes?

"Dylan, I—"

"Say no more. You'd prefer to be friends," he cut me off, obviously hearing the regret in my voice. He sounded chagrined, which made me feel bad.

"No, it's not that. It's just . . ." I sighed. "I'm not ready for a relationship."

"I understand, but I'd still like to hang out sometimes, if you're up for it?"

"Yes, of course. You know I've always loved your company."

"Great, so I'll see you tomorrow."

"Yes, Yvonne and I are looking forward to it."

Dylan chuckled. "I don't think any of us are looking forward to it as much as Conor. He's had a big stupid smile on his face since he bumped into you at the apartment."

I grinned. "Oh, don't you worry. Yvonne will be smiling too when she sees him."

"He's at the gym by six every morning," Dylan said. "I can't keep up."

"Bet he gets asked out all the time."

"You could say he's had his share of admirers."

"I can't wait to see Yvonne's reaction. It'll be priceless."

"You think she'd go out with a younger man?"

I considered it. "Maybe."

"We'll just have to see how tomorrow night goes then."

"I feel like a matchmaker," I said, a little giddy.

"You're so fucking cute. Now I've got to get back to work."

"Right, of course. See you tomorrow, Dylan."

"See you tomorrow, Ev."

The next morning, I was doing laundry when I got another call from him. I picked up on the third ring, smiling as I answered, "Hello?"

I heard him exhale, his voice apologetic. "Hi Ev. Listen, I'm sorry to have to do this, but can we take a rain check on tonight? There's some work stuff that's come up and—"

"No worries," I was quick to reply. "We can go some other time."

At the back of my mind, I wondered if this was an excuse. I wondered if he'd thought better of it and decided he didn't want to go through the rigmarole of reconnecting. And I understood. I mean, we lived in different worlds now. I was a bartender and he was the CEO of his own company. I wasn't sure how well our lives would mesh anyway.

Or maybe . . . maybe he walked into his store this morning and got a better offer from the pretty, scarlet-haired Laura. A sliver of jealousy ran through me before I quashed it down.

No, that couldn't be it. He already told me Laura wasn't for him. And Dylan wasn't the type to make up excuses. He told you exactly how he felt. When we were teenagers he'd described himself as honest to a fault.

I think he must've heard the quaver of uncertainty in my voice, because his was reassuring and firm. "Evelyn, there's nothing I'd rather be doing tonight than taking you out. But I've got meetings all day, and there was a mix-up on one of our orders at the shop, so I'm going to have to work tonight to correct it." He paused, sighing again. I imagined him running a hand through his hair.

I chewed on my lip, hesitant when I asked, "Will you be taking a break to eat?"

"Well, sure, but—"

"Then why don't I stop by with food? Say no if you'd rather not, I won't be offended," I went on nervously.

"No, no, that's a great idea," Dylan replied and my nervousness evaporated. "Are you sure it's not too much trouble? I don't want to put you out."

"Of course it isn't. I'd only be sitting at home, scrolling mindlessly through Facebook otherwise."

"You're on Facebook?" he asked, sounding both amused and interested.

"Yep. What kind of self-respecting sad case with no social life would I be if I wasn't?"

"You're none of those things," he chided. "And I ask because I've actually tried to look you up on there a few times but couldn't find you."

Hold up. Dylan was on Facebook? Not only that, he'd tried to find me? Now that was far more interesting. I'd tried to look him up on there, too, but had no luck. I wasn't going to tell him that though.

"Oh, that's probably because I go by E. Flynn instead of Evelyn," I explained.

I heard typing in the background, but didn't think much of it until Dylan asked, "Who's the bloke with the pipe?"

He sounded baffled and I laughed out loud, because he was clearly referring to my very dapper profile picture. "That's Evelyn Waugh. He wrote *Brideshead Revisited*. I couldn't find a decent picture of myself, so I decided to look up the most famous person with the same name as me. Now I tell everyone I was named after him. It's confusing, because anyone who knows my mam knows the woman hasn't read a book in her life."

Dylan laughed softly. "You are so odd."

"And by odd you mean inspired?"

"That is exactly what I mean," he confirmed with a smile in his voice. "Also, I just sent you a friend request."

My phone buzzed then pinged in my ear, announcing I had new notification. "Hmm, not sure if I should accept."

"And why's that?"

"I kinda suspect you're one of those people who vague-books all their petty personal grievances."

Dylan chuckled. "Well, how else am I supposed to let people know to watch their backs because I finally discovered who's my friend and who's my enemy?"

I barked a laugh. "You see. I don't have room for that drama in my life."

Dylan's fond tone spread a warmth through my chest. "I've missed talking with you, Evelyn."

I was silent a moment, not sure how to reply. In the end, I awkwardly ignored what he said entirely, "Do you like Asian food? Yvonne took me to this place that does amazing noodles."

"I love it. Come over around seven and we'll eat."

"Right, see you then," I said and hung up. I set my phone on the countertop and questioned what I was getting myself into. A night out with Yvonne and Conor was one thing, but sharing a meal in the confines of Dylan's office was something else entirely. I'd felt so disappointed when he had to cancel. It made me realise how excited I'd been to spend more time with him.

I wore my hair in a ponytail, alongside some jeans and a long-sleeved top when I made my way to *Dylan* later that evening. It was chilly out, so I wore my long winter coat and a scarf, too. I didn't want to dress up and give Dylan the impression I was after anything other than a friendly, platonic meal with an old friend.

Thankfully, there was no Laura to greet me at the door when I arrived, just a handful of staff closing up for the evening. I nodded to one of them, and Dylan must've told him I was coming, because he didn't stop me from heading upstairs.

I gave a quick knock on his office door and waited until I heard him call, "Come in," before I stepped inside. Dylan sat at his desk, his laptop open and his phone plastered to his ear. I shot him a friendly smile and held up the bag with the food. He smiled back warmly and gestured for me to sit.

I removed my coat and scarf, then began opening the noodle containers while Dylan finished his phone call. When he finally hung up, he rubbed at the space between his eyebrows and let out a weary breath.

"That smells amazing."

I pushed a container towards him. "Stressful day?"

"You could say that. Oh my God, these are delicious." He paused to savour the food then continued. "Laura ordered several hundred units of the wrong scent from our factory in California. *E.V.* is our most popular product, but we're completely out of stock until the new order arrives. I might've lost my temper a little with her over it," he admitted, sounding regretful.

"Oh," I frowned. "Is she okay?"

He rubbed his jaw. "She cried. It was . . . uncomfortable."

Man, now I felt bad for her. I'd never cried in front of a boss before, but there had been times when I'd come close, so I definitely empathised. Then again, she and Dylan didn't have the most conventional employer-employee relationship, which sort of added a whole extra layer of awkwardness.

"Did you apologise?"

"Yes. Then I suggested she take the rest of the day off, which is why I had to cancel our dinner."

"Big softie."

"Tell me about it. I should've just told her to chin up and get on with things."

"That might've made her cry more."

"Which is exactly why I didn't do it. Anyway, let's not talk about work. How are you?" He lifted another forkful of noodles to his mouth and ate.

I shrugged. "It's my day off, so I did laundry and watched TV, because you know, I'm one of those exciting, creative types."

Dylan chuckled. "You self-deprecate, but you are creative. Remember your allotment? All those flowers were like your art."

I stiffened and twisted some noodles around my fork. "Yeah well, like I said, I don't do that anymore."

"You really should think about getting back into it. There are lots of flower farms outside the city."

I shook my head. "Dylan, I know your heart's in the right place and all, but don't waste your energy trying to convince me to garden again. It won't work."

He studied me. "And why not?"

"Because I said goodbye to it a long time ago. After Sam died, that part of me went with him."

Dylan flinched visibly at the mention of our lost friend.

"Wow," I breathed as I came to a realisation. *Surely he doesn't . . .* "You still blame yourself."

He didn't meet my gaze, the only sign of his discomfort his throat moving as he swallowed. "Some things are hard to let go of," he said finally.

"Yes, but if you don't, you'll die with them hanging over your head. It took a long time for me to get over Sam's death. I mean, I'll never fully be over it, because I think about him every day, but I'm not letting it rule me anymore. Or at least I'm trying not to."

"What made you decide that?" Dylan asked with interest.

I ate more noodles, my eyes resting on the dark wood of his desk. "Just something Gran said to me before she died." I paused and glanced up at him. His attentive gaze urged me to continue.

"It's funny, but even before she died, I think she knew she wasn't long for the world. She told me that once she was gone, I wouldn't have any more excuses. I asked her what she meant, angry at how she was so accepting of her fate. She said I used my love for her as an excuse not to live my life. I told her she was being ridiculous, that I was living my life just fine. She shook her head and said, *No love, how can you be with that dark cloud hanging over your head? When I'm gone you'll have no other choice but to find the sun.*"

"Poetic," Dylan mused, absorbed by my story.

I inhaled a deep breath, scraping my fork around in the container. "And then when she did die, I stood by her grave and thought, *No, Gran, you were wrong. I can't find the sun, because the clouds have gotten so much thicker*. But then days turned into weeks. I was alone in our flat, and suddenly, I couldn't stand to live there anymore. The place was too quiet, and everything in it made me sad just to look at. I felt lonely. So, when Yvonne made her offer for me to come and live with her, like she did every month, I finally said yes. Gran was right all along. She knew I couldn't stand to be without a purpose, and without her I didn't have one. I decided if she was right about that, then maybe she was right about me finding the sun, too. Maybe I should finally just . . . you know, *try* to be happy. Try to be the girl I was before I lost Sam."

When I finished speaking, Dylan's eyes were misty. I stiffened, uncomfortable with his show of emotion, and also because I'd revealed far more than I intended. He blinked and the glossiness disappeared.

"I hope you succeed," he said, then focused on eating his food.

We ate in quiet for a while, both of us almost finished when his phone rang. He shot me an apologetic look. "I'm sorry, I have to take this."

I waved away his apology. "No, go ahead."

He held the phone to his ear while I slurped down the last of my noodles and listened to his side of the conversation. "Hello?" A pause.

"Yes, that's correct." Another pause.

"And to confirm, we need eight hundred bottles of *E.V.*, five hundred *Synaesthesia*, and three hundred *Limerence*. When is your estimated delivery?"

"Next Tuesday? Perfect. Yes, talk soon."

He put the phone down and fiddled with his shirt collar. "The order all fixed then?" I asked, amused by how business-like and professional he was on the phone.

Dylan sighed. "Yes, but the business we'll lose over the next few days still makes me break out in hives. My poor floor staff will have an awful time explaining to people that *E.V.* is out of stock."

I arched an intrigued brow. "That was your first perfume, right?" He nodded. "And it's still the most popular?"

"It's a timeless scent," he replied and looked at me speculatively. "I created it at a time when I was most inspired to make something meaningful."

"Oh," I replied, wiping my mouth with a napkin and gathering our used utensils.

I sensed Dylan studying me before he stated, disbelieving, "You've never smelled it, have you?"

I met his gaze and shook my head, sheepish when I admitted, "Dylan, the other day when I tried *Wildflower,* that was the first time I'd ever smelled one of your perfumes."

There was a long moment of silence. Dylan's eyes betrayed his emotions. He almost appeared . . . offended. No, that wasn't the right word. Hurt. He was hurt I'd never taken it upon myself to try his scents.

"You look surprised."

He frowned and glanced away. "I'm not surprised, it's just . . ."

"What?" I leaned forward in my chair.

He rubbed his mouth with his fingers and stood up. He paced the room then came to stand in front of me. It looked like it took a lot for him to say his next words.

"Each time I release a new perfume, I always imagine we're having a conversation."

"You and me?" I was taken aback.

"Yes." His voice was passionate. "I think of you going into a store and trying it on. I amuse myself wondering what you think, which products are your favourite." He shook his head. "Were you not even a little bit curious?"

More than anything.

"Of course I was curious, but I was already so jealous of everything you'd achieved. I guess I didn't want to know how amazing your perfumes were, because it would only make me feel like more of a failure."

"That's ridiculous. You're not a failure."

I huffed a self-deprecating breath. "Tell that to my bank account."

"Evelyn, if it weren't for your influence, I might never have become what I am today. You do realise that, don't you?"

I flushed and stared at my hands, unsure how to respond. Dylan moved about the room, going to different shelves and plucking out various bottles.

"What are you doing?"

"Introducing you to a world you helped create," he replied with fervour. I watched as he placed each bottle in front of me, then opened the scent named *Synaesthesia*. He knelt before me, took my hand, then turned it over to expose my wrist. He gave a soft spritz and fresh jasmine assaulted my senses, plunging me into memory. It had always been one of my favourite flowers to grow, had seemed so exotic and pretty in a place that was neither.

"When we were teenagers, you sometimes smelled like jasmine," Dylan said. "Then you told me how you liked to make jasmine water in the mornings. When I smell this scent, I think of you pottering around your flat, watering your plants and putting the kettle on for tea."

"It's beautiful," I breathed, overly aware of Dylan's fingers that still circled my wrist. It was hard to get my head around the fact that my humdrum, mundane existence inspired a perfume thousands of women around the world wore every day.

He plucked up another bottle, *Hiraeth*, uncapped it and sprayed it on my other wrist. I inhaled and closed my eyes. It smelled like a rainforest; I could literally feel the fat drops of water hit my face, run down my neck and pool at the base of my spine.

"Remember that weekend I came back to Dublin for Conor's graduation?" Dylan murmured. His eyes traced the line of my wrist, ran up my arm to rest on my face. "You got caught in the rain."

"It was pouring down," I added, falling through the rabbit hole of memory. "And then you just appeared."

His eyes sparkled, his smile intense when he said, "That day was when *Hiraeth* was born."

Six

Eight years ago

I stood by the bus stop in the rain, no other choice but to get soaked. I made the mistake of leaving the house without an umbrella, so it was my own fault really. It was rush hour, and the shelter was already full of people huddled under, trying not to get wet.

Currently, I was working as a supermarket cashier. It wasn't the most exciting job in the world, but at least I got a discount on groceries.

Yeah, not very glamourous, but life wasn't glamourous, not for the *hoi polloi*. Weirdly, I used to think that meant the upper classes, then Yvonne told me it was Greek for the common people, the rank and file. I guessed, because it sounded a little like 'high people' I made the wrong assumption.

Anyway, that was me. Your average worker bee, plodding her way through life, dissatisfied and a little sad, but not dissatisfied and sad enough to make a change. To be honest, happiness seemed like a lie made up by fairy tales and self-help books. Now my eyes were open to all the dark corners that hovered around the light.

Like the dementors in *Harry Potter*, they waited for their chance to swallow you up. That's why I didn't bother trying for anything good. Good things were only taken away.

Like Sam.

I shook myself out of my dreary thoughts and wriggled my toes around in my soaked shoes. I looked forward to stripping off and sinking into a nice, warm bath as soon as I got home. Yvonne worked tonight, so I'd have the place to myself. I'd pop a ready meal in the microwave, and maybe even open a bottle of wine . . .

"Evelyn?"

I blinked, distracted from my plans for the evening when I heard my name. I glanced up and my jaw dropped. *Dylan?* He held a large black umbrella and wore a dark winter coat and woollen hat. It was hard to make him out past the fat drops of rain obscuring my vision. They pooled in my eyebrows and fell into my eyes.

I blinked some more and stared at him. I hadn't seen him in over three years. When he first left for the U.S., he'd sent monthly letters keeping me updated on how things were going. It was so Dylan to do something completely old school like that. Still, I never wrote back. I knew it sounded cruel, but staying in touch only prolonged the pain for both of us. Eventually, he got the message and quit writing.

In a way, I was disappointed.

In another way, I was relieved.

No contact was so much better than getting sneak peeks of his new life and feeling down that I wasn't with him.

Finally, I managed to get some words out. "Dylan, my goodness, what a surprise."

He lifted a thumb and pointed over his shoulder. "Yeah, I'm, uh, staying at the hotel across the street. It's great to see you."

"You, too," I breathed, though great wasn't the right word. Startled was a better one. The hotel he pointed to didn't look so fancy. In fact, it was downtrodden and old, the brickwork in need of a new paint job. Maybe life wasn't going as successfully for Dylan as I often imagined it was.

His gaze followed mine and he grimaced. "It's not as bad as it looks."

"Hey, I still live at the Villas. I'm in no position to judge."

His lips twitched as his gaze travelled down my drenched body and back up. I was overly aware of the raindrop that sat at the tip of my nose. I wanted to wipe it away, but I was too self-conscious to do it with Dylan staring at me.

When I didn't speak again he said, "Aren't you going to ask what I'm doing here?"

No, Dylan, I'm not, because I'm too embarrassed to be standing here in the lashing rain, wearing my cashier's uniform, cheap shoes, and name tag.

I felt so small. Why did you bump into old flames when you looked your absolute worst? It was one of God's twisted celestial algorithms that made it happen to everyone at least once in their lives.

I cleared my scratchy throat and asked what he wanted me to ask. "What are you doing here?"

Dylan smiled, completely at ease. He didn't look at all uncomfortable or frazzled like I was sure I did, even with the fact that he was staying in a crappy hotel. He stepped closer so that his umbrella sheltered me, an unexpected and kind gesture. "I came back to visit Dad," he replied. "He's still living in Galway with his brother, got a job down there and everything. I took the train here last night."

"Are you staying long?" I questioned further, curious now.

He shoved one hand in his pocket. "Just for another two days. It's Conor's college graduation tomorrow, so I thought I'd kill two birds with one stone." He paused, handsome eyes grazing my features. "And of course, I was going to come pay you a visit."

"You were?"

"Why wouldn't I?"

I swallowed, feeling guilty. "I just thought, since I never replied to your letters—"

"Ev, I understand why you didn't write," he said, eyes full of compassion.

But it still hurt, didn't it?

It certainly hurt me not to reply. I cleared my throat and stared up at him. "Yes, well, I hope everything's going well for you in LA. I mean, you've got a tan now, so it must be going okay at least," I teased, trying to lighten the mood.

"Why don't we go over to my hotel, and I'll make you some tea. We can have a catch up?"

The offer took me by surprise, and I glanced around for a better option. Strangely, I did want to catch up. I just didn't want to do it in the confines of what was sure to be a tiny hotel room. "How about we go to the café down the street instead?" I suggested and pointed a few buildings down.

Dylan's cheeks coloured as he realised how his invitation sounded. "Right, yes, sorry, let's go to the café," he said and offered me his arm.

I linked mine through his and internally freaked out at how close we were. I could smell his cologne, faint as it was. When we reached the café, Dylan shook out his umbrella and left it by the door. I quickly excused myself to the bathroom to dry off and have a private little freak out.

He looks as gorgeous as ever.

You look like a drowned rat.

But he's staying in that hotel.

He can't be doing that well for himself.

And it's not like I need to care what I look like.

We're not together anymore, nor will we be ever again.

Just go out there, chat like a normal person, and wish him well with the rest of his life.

When I returned, Dylan sat at a table reading the menu. I lowered myself into a chair and clasped my hands together. "So—"

"What can I get you two?" a waitress interrupted, and I flushed for no apparent reason.

"I'll have tea," Dylan answered.

"Yes, tea for me, too," I said, then added, "Oh, and a scone, please."

The waitress left and I looked back to Dylan. "They have really nice scones here."

He smiled. "I'll remember that for next time."

"Was the flight awful? It must be terribly long to come from California," I said. If I just kept asking mundane questions, maybe I'd relax more.

"It was a little under eleven hours, but I kept busy. Boredom is the real challenge on long flights."

"Did you watch any movies? I hear they have TV screens on the seat in front of you with a choice of films." Dylan's gaze softened. He must've thought me terribly quaint now that he was living over there, but I couldn't help my curiosity. I'd never been on a long-haul flight.

"Yeah, there are screens. I prefer to bring a good book with me though. If I start reading at the beginning of the flight, I can be almost finished by the time I arrive at my destination."

"What did you read?"

"The new Stephen King."

"Oh, I heard that's a real page turner."

Dylan nodded. "I enjoyed it."

Silence fell and I scrambled for something else to say. The waitress came with our order, and I busied myself spreading jam on my scone.

"How's Yvonne and your gran?" Dylan asked, eyes never leaving me. I was distinctly irritated by how much more relaxed he was.

"Yvonne's good. She's going to New York in the summer. Gran is as good as can be expected, but I'm starting to feel like the home's not a good fit for her anymore. I'm considering having her move in with me after Yvonne leaves, but I still need to figure out the logistics."

Dylan's brows furrowed. "Won't that be a lot of work?"

"There's a carer's allowance I can apply for so I can care for her full-time."

"Those allowances are notoriously low, Ev."

"Well, I don't mind that. So long as we have enough to get by."

His brows furrowed even deeper and I got the sense he wanted to say something but was holding back.

"What?" I asked.

Dylan looked out the window a moment then back to me. "I just think you can do better."

"Who's to say caring isn't doing better? It's one of the most important jobs a person can commit to. It's society's fault for belittling it and making it so low paid."

His expression gentled. "No, you're right. I'm sorry for saying that."

I frowned and clasped my hands around my teacup. "Anyway, tell me about LA. Is it everything you hoped it would be?"

He rubbed his jaw. "It's certainly different. I knew it was going to be hard over there, but I may have underestimated just how difficult. I'm trying to start my own business, and I'm full of ideas, but getting together the start-up capital has been tricky."

"Oh, I'm sure you'll convince some banker to lend you the money."

Dylan's eyes crinkled in a smile. "It's a little more complicated than that."

"You'll figure it out."

"Great pep talk."

"You're welcome." I grinned and ate a bite of my scone.

We were quiet for a little while, just letting the sounds of the busy café wash over us. I couldn't stop looking at him every chance I got. I was fixated by the way his tight-fitting jumper hugged his arms, how his sandy hair curled at the temples. When he caught me looking, I flushed and fiddled with my napkin.

"Why don't you come with me to Conor's tomorrow night? He and some of his college roommates are having a party at their flat to celebrate graduating."

I shook my head. "Oh, no I couldn't—"

"Ev, I'm leaving in two days, and who knows when I'll be back to visit again. It could be years. Just give me one night."

Man, he was hard to resist, especially with those gorgeous eyes of his pleading with me to say yes. I exhaled. "I don't get off work until eight tomorrow."

"Eight is fine. I'll pick you up outside."

"How do you know—?"

He motioned to my name tag, which had the name of the supermarket at the top. Right. I let out another long breath. "Okay, but I can't stay long."

"We'll be there three hours, tops," he said, smiling wide because he'd won me over.

"*Two* hours," I corrected and stood, pulling out some money to pay for my tea and scone. "I'll see you tomorrow."

Dylan lounged back, his expression effortlessly sexy as he watched me go. "See you tomorrow, Evelyn."

What, oh what was I getting myself into?

***

I brought a change of clothes to work with me, hoping to have enough time to change and do my make-up before Dylan arrived to pick me up. I was about two hours into my shift when I saw him walk through the sliding glass doors. What the hell was he doing here already? It was only three o'clock.

I continued to scan items, watching him before he noticed me. He looked around, eyes skimming the newspaper headlines before they headed my direction. My breath caught, and in that moment I knew. *I was in trouble.* I was so determined to keep my emotions out of this unexpected reunion, but I couldn't help it. My heart beat fast and my palms tingled just remembering how I'd linked my arm through his yesterday. How without a word he'd sheltered me from the rain with his umbrella. It was little gestures like those that were just so Dylan.

He waited until I was done with my customer to approach, his smile sheepish. "I know we agreed eight o'clock, but I just wanted to stop by and bring you this." He held out a takeaway cup and a paper bag. I took both items shyly and opened the bag. It was tea and one of the same scones I'd had yesterday.

Flutters invaded my insides.

It was a simple gesture, but it really got to me. Maybe because my life had been devoid of any kind gestures for a while now.

"Thank you," I said quietly.

God, was I going to cry? I needed to get my shit together.

Dylan shoved his hands in his pockets, eyes intent on mine. "Right, well, I guess I'll see you later then."

I nodded. "Yep, see you later."

I held my breath until he walked out the door. Michelle, one of my co-workers at the next till, shot me a grin, "That your boyfriend?"

"Ex," I said.

She let out a low whistle. "If I had a fella who looked like that I wouldn't have let him go for all the tea in China."

No, Michelle, I don't believe you would.

Sometimes, unfortunately, you had to do away with selfishness and let people go, for their own sake if nothing else. I sipped on my tea and continued taking customers, saving the scone for my break.

Later on, while slipping into a little black dress and heels in the bathroom next to the staff locker room, I wondered if I should just cancel. I was nervous for two reasons. One, because at the age of twenty-one, I'd never actually been to a college party, and two, because I was in danger of doing something silly if I had too much to drink.

Like kissing my ex-boyfriend.

Probably best to stick to Coke tonight.

I let my hair down and put on some make-up. When I was done, I shoved the rest of my things in my locker and put on my coat. The night-time chill tickled at my ears and the tip of my nose when I stepped outside. Dylan stood next to a lamppost waiting for me, handsome as ever.

"You look beautiful," he breathed.

I swallowed a lump of nerves. "You haven't even seen my outfit yet."

He shook his head. "Don't need to."

I wasn't sure how to reply, so I simply rubbed my hands together and glanced down the street.

"I thought we'd take a taxi," Dylan said as he came and took my arm, linking it through his just like yesterday.

"S-sounds good."

A few minutes later, we sat next to each other in the back seat, neither one of us speaking. I focused on the lights of the city rushing by and not on the fact that Dylan's hand rested on the seat, mere inches from mine. This felt so odd. Three years ago, we saw each other every single day, but then he was gone. It was hard to adjust to being around him, especially since he was leaving tomorrow.

It made me unreasonably sad.

My heart wished for a world where he brought me tea and scones at work every day, where I got to wear nice clothes and get taken to parties. But my head knew it would never be with Dylan. Maybe with some other guy, but not with him.

Dylan still had so much to achieve. I could feel it.

We arrived outside a house in Portobello and headed inside. The front door was already open, people idling in the hallway and staircase, music playing from a speaker somewhere inside. I didn't know anyone, so I stood close to Dylan. He must've sensed my nervousness, because he silently slid his fingers through mine and held my hand. I glanced at him, and a whoosh of air fled my lungs. Dylan's gaze was full of tenderness. It felt like a lifetime ago that he last looked at me that way.

"Dylan!" came a familiar voice, and Conor emerged from the kitchen into the hallway. He looked about the same as the last time I saw him, though admittedly he didn't hang around the Villas much anymore. He was a college student now, had all his college student buddies to hang out with. He wore the remnants of a suit, jacket gone, tie askew. It was clear he'd already had a few drinks, judging by his crooked, tipsy smile.

"Hey, where's your gown?" Dylan teased. "Are you sure you graduated?"

"You only rent them, you don't take them home with you," Conor slurred. He stepped forward and pulled Dylan into a hug, causing him to lose grip on my hand.

"It's so great to see you!"

"Great to see you, too," Dylan said with a chuckle as he patted Conor on the back.

Conor's attention came to me, his smile huge. "And Evelyn's here. It's been ages." Then to Dylan, "So, you went straight to her place, huh?"

Dylan widened his eyes meaningfully at Conor and carefully cleared his throat. "No, we actually bumped into each other in town."

"Oh, but remember on the phone you said—"

"Why don't you show me and Ev where the drinks are," Dylan interrupted, and I wondered what was up.

"Keg's this way," Conor replied, and we followed him into the kitchen. After he supplied us both with beers, he went to do the rounds with the rest of the partygoers, leaving me and Dylan alone. We stood in a corner of the kitchen, which was quieter than the rest of the house.

"So," I said, glancing around. "This is what college life looks like."

Dylan arched a brow. "First impressions?"

"A lot messier than I imagined."

"Five blokes live here," he replied, as though that explained it.

"Not all men are messy. I remember your bedroom used to be so neat and tidy."

Dylan arched a brow and smirked. "You remember my bedroom, eh?"

I flushed, because we'd spent quite a few evenings making out in there . . . and other stuff. I punched him gently on the arm. "Don't."

Dylan tipped his beer to his mouth and winked. "Can't help it. Good memories."

My tummy fizzled, but I didn't respond. After a second I asked, "What did Conor mean about you coming straight to my place?"

His expression sobered. "I was hoping you didn't catch that."

"Why?"

He seemed edgy, red tinting his cheeks. "Visiting my dad and Conor wasn't the main reason I came back, Ev."

My chest ached at his confession. I asked a question, but was pretty sure I already knew the answer. "What was the main reason?"

He looked all about the room, not meeting my eyes when he spoke. "To see you."

My heart pounded at his quiet intensity. "Oh."

He turned, stepping closer to me. My back hit the wall. "I was hoping you'd feel differently than you did three years ago."

"Differently?" I whispered. He was so close now, and his breath on my skin made it tingle. I wanted to touch him, run my hands across the solid lines of his shoulders. Instead, I stayed completely still.

"I want you to come back with me," he breathed, eyes flickering between mine, searching. He exhaled heavily. "But I know you won't."

Not *won't*, Dylan. *Can't.*

I frowned and chewed on my lip. "I'm, um, just going to use the bathroom." I had to get out of there for a minute.

He caught me by the elbow. "Are you leaving?"

"No, of course not. I just need a minute."

He studied me, then let go. "Okay. Take your time."

I went upstairs and found the bathroom occupied. I slumped against the wall, because I didn't really need to go anyway. *Dylan came back for me.* Three years ago, I told him to never come back. I was grieving and emotional, and I didn't really mean it. In all honesty, I felt over the moon that he still wanted me. But it was pointless. I couldn't go to America just as much as I couldn't three years ago.

When I went back downstairs, Dylan was in the living room. He sat on the couch, still nursing his beer. I sat on the arm next to him, because there were two guys on the other side having a deep and very drunken conversation. I could tell by how loud they were being.

"Hey," I murmured.

"Hey," he replied, eyes finding mine.

"Can we just—"

"Listen, Ev—"

We both spoke at once. I exhaled and looked at him kindly, starting over. "You're leaving tomorrow. Let's just enjoy tonight, okay? No worries, no obligations, just, you know, appreciate each other's company."

Dylan smiled and reached out to take my hand. He wrapped his fingers around mine, squeezing tight. "Sounds good to me."

I didn't have anywhere to sit, so I stayed on the arm of the chair. I didn't drink any more alcohol, because with how I was feeling, I knew it was a bad idea to get drunk. Then three of Conor's friends came into the room and began performing a comedy skit for everyone. Apparently, they were a comedy trio in their spare time. The skit was actually pretty funny, and at one point I was in a fit of laughter. I wiped a tear from my eye and glanced over at Dylan to see if he was laughing, too.

He wasn't.

His attention was so fixed on me. I might as well have been the only person in the room. His smile was intimate, and he reached out to take my hand. He pulled me over to sit on his lap, and I stiffened.

His hand covered my knee as he whispered in my ear, "Just for tonight, Ev."

Okay, Dylan, just for tonight.

For the next hour or so, we didn't speak much. Conor's college friends were far too entertaining, so there wasn't much need for conversation. Dylan wrapped his arms around my waist, his thumb brushing at the fabric of my dress. Tingles skittered down my spine, while Conor dropped down next to us, drunkenly telling us all about the master's programme he'd gotten into like it was the most interesting thing in the world. He barely noticed how Dylan was making subtle work of seducing me in a melting pile of goo.

Just being close to him, his breath on my neck, was enough to arouse me to stratospheric levels.

Despite all the heightened sexual tension, I did actually manage to have a good time. It felt like the first time in forever that I'd just allowed myself to enjoy something.

It was around midnight when Dylan went to grab our coats. He called a taxi, and we said our goodbyes to Conor.

"Two stops, please," I said to the driver as we slid in the back.

Dylan's hotel was the first stop. He'd been quiet on the drive, and I wondered if he felt sad that our brief time was over, because I knew I did. When the taxi stopped outside his hotel, he softly gripped my hand and said, "Come up. Just for a little bit."

Wordlessly, I nodded. I wasn't ready to say goodbye. Not yet. Dylan paid the driver and helped me out. We were both silent as we ascended in the hotel's rickety lift. Reaching Dylan's floor, I stepped out and he led me down the hall. As expected, his room was tiny. There was a bed, a dresser, and a TV in the far corner.

I stood by the bed, unsure if I should take off my coat. Dylan took his off then turned to look at me. His eyes traced my features, lingering for too long on my lips. If he didn't stop staring at me like that, I was going to kiss him.

He stepped closer and with careful fingers unzipped my coat and slid it down my shoulders. He threw it on the bed and took a second to just . . . take me in. All pretences were gone. We both knew I hadn't come up here for tea and friendly conversation.

He brought his hand to my neck, sliding up to cup my jaw. I exhaled heavily at his touch, and then his mouth was on mine, lips caressing my lips. I moaned when he slid his tongue inside, and suddenly we were on the bed. Dylan braced himself above me, both of us full of need. He ran his hand down the side of my body then pushed my skirt up to my belly. He swiftly unbuckled his belt and opened his fly. I grasped at his pants, pushing them down.

"Are you on the pill?" he asked breathlessly.

I nodded. "Yes, but we still need—"

"I haven't been with anyone since you," he blurted and I froze, stunned.

I hadn't been with anyone either. I only stayed on the pill because it helped with my periods, but Dylan . . .

A lone, unexpected tear ran down my cheek as I whispered, "Me neither."

Dylan's expression mirrored my own. What a fine pair we made. Everything had been so wonderfully effortless between us, so perfect that we'd ruined each other for anyone else. Without another word, he pulled my underwear down just enough and pushed inside me. I gasped at how he filled me and closed my eyes to bury my face in his neck. Dylan's thrusts were hard and fast, somehow fucking me and making love to me all at once.

His mouth found mine, and he kissed me with so much passion I felt like I might burst with it. He broke the kiss and held my eyes when he came.

He was so bloody beautiful.

"I love you, Ev," he breathed.

That was it. He was going to break me. More tears streamed down my face. Dylan made soothing noises, kissed away my tears. By the time morning light streamed through the curtains, I was certain he'd kissed every inch of my body. I lay next to him, the sounds of his deep breathing filling the room as he slept, and knew I had to leave.

Last night had been the perfect goodbye. I didn't want to sully it with an awkward, possibly regretful morning after. As quietly as I could manage, I climbed out of bed and got dressed. I stared at Dylan while he slept and knew there was something I needed to say to him. I just didn't have the courage to do it in person.

There was no paper in the room, no pens either. I managed to find a pencil and an unused envelope in my bag. On the back of the envelope, I wrote a message.

Dylan,

Last night was beautiful. Thank you for giving that to me. As I'm writing this, I miss you already, and you're so close to me, fast asleep. I want to tell you that I think you're incredible. You're clever and talented and caring and people deserve to know you. So please, don't hang on to the past. When you go back to LA, start living your life, meet people, get laid, make mistakes, and fall in love.

And if you won't do it for yourself, do it for me.

Love always,

Evelyn.

I blinked and a tear fell down, staining the paper. I placed the note on the dresser, then quietly left the room. When I got outside, the cold morning air assaulted me, and my heart felt like someone had beaten it with a meat tenderiser. The bus driver gave me a funny look, as I hopped on the 151 that would take me home, my face red from crying. I'd meant everything I said in that note, and now I truly knew how it felt to do something selfless.

Because letting Dylan go a second time was the most painful, heartbreaking thing in the world.

Seven

Present

Monday   10:34   dylanod@dylanscents.com   to evflynn21@gmail.com

You up to much today?

Monday   10:41   evflynn21@gmail.com   to dylanod@dylanscents

Not really. Just working on my screenplay ;-)

Monday   10:44   dylanod@dylanscents.com   to evflynn21@gmail.com

Is it raunchy? The winky face infers raunchiness.

Monday   10:46   evflynn21@gmail.com   to dylanod@dylanscents

Nah, it's about two dudes who work in an HMV.

Monday   10:47   dylanod@dylanscents.com   to evflynn21@gmail.com

Okay. I'm hooked.

Monday   10:53   evflynn21@gmail.com   to dylanod@dylanscents

So, their names are Johnny and Eddy. Eddy's the nerdy one. He has a crush on this girl who comes into the store sometimes. Her name's Vanessa, but she already has a boyfriend and won't give Eddy the time of day.

Monday   10:56   dylanod@dylanscents.com   to evflynn21@gmail.com

Poor Eddy.

Monday   11:00   evflynn21@gmail.com   to dylanod@dylanscents

I know. Johnny's the cool one, but dumb as a stump. Everybody likes him even though he's always slapping girls on the arse and calling them sugartits. Anyhoo, one day, Johnny and Eddy are in the storage room and they find this dusty old VCR player with a videotape inside. They press play, but all they get is a squiggly static screen. The fuzzy sound gets really loud and then all of a sudden, they're transported back to the 1500s. They're still in their HMV uniforms, so everyone's looking at them funny.

Monday 11:02 dylanod@dylanscents.com to evflynn21@gmail.com

Well, of course.

Monday 11:08 evflynn21@gmail.com to dylanod@dylanscents

Luckily for them, they're already in the market place, so they steal some clothes from a merchant's stall. The guy spots them right as they're walking away and starts shaking his fist in anger. They run off then bump into this girl who, get this, looks exactly like Vanessa.

Monday 11:12 dylanod@dylanscents.com to evflynn21@gmail.com

SHUT UP.

Monday 11:16 evflynn21@gmail.com to dylanod@dylanscents

Yep. Only her name isn't Vanessa. It's *Shan*essa. To Eddy's delight, she fancies him right away and wants to get married. But then Johnny's all, *sorry, babe, he can't marry you. We have to get back to our own time period.* Eddy's like, *how the hell are we* *supposed to do that?* Johnny goes, *it's simple. We need to find Leonardo da Vinci. He'll build us a time machine, so we can go back home.* Conveniently, they're already in Italy.

Monday 11:20 dylanod@dylanscents.com to evflynn21@gmail.com

I question Johnny's knowledge of Leonardo da Vinci . . .

Monday 11:24 evflynn21@gmail.com to dylanod@dylanscents

He watched a documentary once. But anyway, before Da Vinci come the hijinks. They wind up fighting a duel with a medieval knight to defend the honour of a fair maiden. They also attend an audience with the king, and convince him to charge his people less tax. They even set Shanessa up with a guy they meet who, get this, looks exactly like Eddy.

Monday 11:27 dylanod@dylanscents.com to evflynn21@gmail.com

Okay, now I'm dubious.

Monday 11:32 evflynn21@gmail.com to dylanod@dylanscents

No really. It's perfectly logical. So, after all these good deeds, they finally go on their journey to find old Leo. Cue the fun montage. He turns out to be a kindly old gent who's more than happy to invent their time machine. When they get home, Eddy has a newfound confidence that has Vanessa eyeing him lustily. She drops her boyfriend and they ride off into the sunset.

Monday 11:36 dylanod@dylanscents.com to evflynn21@gmail.com

What about Johnny?

Monday   11:41   evflynn21@gmail.com   to dylanod@dylanscents

Johnny's still dumb as rocks, but he's a real popular guy, so life is good. The movie ends with him trying to peek down some girl's blouse and she slaps him across the face. Everybody's like *typical Johnny* and they get a real good chuckle out of it. Roll end credits.

Monday   10:56   dylanod@dylanscents.com   to evflynn21@gmail.com

Man, if this was 1989, that script would've sold like hotcakes.

Monday   11:10   evflynn21@gmail.com   to dylanod@dylanscents

I know, right?

***

That was just one of many conversations I'd had with Dylan over the last two weeks. It was so weird to be able to message him whenever I felt like it and we could shoot the shit. Talk about any random crap that came into our heads. It was nice to be silly sometimes, and it was really helping me focus on the positive. Life didn't always have to be so serious and dark. It could be ridiculous and funny and generally pleasant.

After the meal we shared in his office, I hadn't seen Dylan in person. He was always so busy, but tonight we were finally going out. He, Yvonne, Conor, and I. Since we'd only been communicating electronically, I was both nervous and excited to see him in person.

"Do you know where they're taking us?" Yvonne asked as I sat by her dresser putting make-up on. My room, which was more of a glorified storage closet, didn't have space for such luxuries.

"I'm not sure."

"Do you think I should wear my red dress?"

"Yeah, go for it."

"It's not too risqué?"

"No, you look gorgeous in it," I said, attempting to reassure her. Yvonne was always indecisive when it came to clothes. She didn't like to look like she was on display, which I completely understood, but still. At thirty-nine, she was even more attractive than she'd been in her twenties. I guess being a non-smoker and a very light drinker all your life paid off.

"Okay, I'm going to wear it," she decided, steeling herself.

I smiled at her through the mirror, happy with my make-up, then got up to put on my own outfit. I wore my best pair of jeans with a loose, flowy cream blouse and some heels. I thought it was smart enough to work for a range of possibilities.

I'd just finished pinning my hair up when the buzzer went. Yvonne hurried over to answer it. "Hello."

"Yvonne, it's Dylan. Can we come up?"

"Sure, I'll buzz you in now," she replied and my stomach tightened. I was excited like a giddy teen.

The front door opened and in walked Dylan and Conor. They were both going casual in jeans and shirts, which put me at ease somewhat. My attention rested on Dylan the longest. What he said about me growing into my face suddenly made sense, because he'd grown into his, too. He looked comfortable in his own skin now.

He'd achieved everything he'd set out to, and there was contentment where once there'd been restlessness and dissatisfaction.

"Hi," I said, going to give Conor a quick hug and then Dylan. He held me tight for a beat longer than normal, murmuring in my ear, "You look amazing."

"Thanks," I replied and stood back as Yvonne came out of her room, bag in hand.

"Hi everyone," she said, all smiles. When she saw Conor she stopped short, blinked several times then cleared her throat. Quickly, she gathered herself and stepped forward. "Dylan, it's good to see you again. And C-Conor, it's been a long time." She cast me a quick glance as if to say, *holy shite, he grew up, didn't he?*

"Too long," he agreed. "Hello, Yvonne." He smiled, eyes wandering over her appreciatively. *And there it was. Holy crap.* It was hard to believe that even after all these years, he still had a thing for her. I guess we always held a candle for our first crush, which was probably why Dylan had such a potent effect on me.

A moment passed between us, like nobody knew what to say.

"Well, let's get going, shall we?" I ventured and Dylan nodded.

"We have a taxi waiting outside."

"Oh great," Yvonne said. "I always have such trouble flagging them down. It's like I'm invisible."

"It's 'cause you've got shaky hands," I said, teasing. "Those taxi drivers can spot weakness a mile off."

"Oh, it's a cutthroat business hailing taxis in NYC," Conor agreed. "They can sniff out blood in the water like nobody's business."

Yvonne chuckled. "Right. Maybe there's a class I can go to."

"Of course, there is. There's a class for everything here," I said.

"The land of miracles," Dylan added with a wink. It was something I said to him the other week, and it made me smile that he remembered.

"Exactly," I said as he opened the door to the taxi and ushered me in. Conor did the same for Yvonne on the other side, and I might've been mistaken, but I thought her cheeks reddened ever so slightly.

It was a tight squeeze, with my leg resting right next to Dylan's during the ride. His attention wandered to where our knees met; he focused on the contact for a second before directing his attention out the window.

I had butterflies the entire journey.

Our destination turned out to be a cheesy but completely fabulous Irish-themed pub. There were pictures of shamrocks and leprechauns above the door, and all the woodwork was painted bright emerald green.

"We thought you might appreciate some kitsch," Conor said, grinning as we walked inside. Surprisingly, the place was packed, and there was a trad band on stage playing a set.

"Oh, wow. It's so bad it's almost good."

"It might be garish, but they do the best pub grub in the city. Conor and I come here all the time when we get homesick," said Dylan.

"I can smell the bacon and cabbage already," Yvonne added. "Come on, let's grab a table."

We found a free booth in the back, far enough away from the live music that we could carry out a decent conversation. I sat down first, and Dylan slid in next to me, leaving Yvonne and Conor to share the seat on the other side. I picked up the menu and perused the options.

"So, how are you liking the city?" Yvonne asked, making conversation. I knew I was letting the side down, but Dylan wouldn't stop looking at me, and I felt self-conscious. *What was he thinking?*

"I love it," Conor replied. "I'm actually thinking of buying an apartment here and making it my base. I still need to travel between the stores a couple times a year, but *Dylan NY* has by far been our most successful opening. If we're lucky, we might even be able to open another branch next year."

"Two perfume shops in one city?" Yvonne said, wide-eyed. "I'm impressed. Oh, and I forgot to say, I saw your full-page advertisement in *The Times* yesterday. It was very eye-catching."

"Thanks," Conor said. "But the concept was Dylan's."

"What was the picture?" I asked, curious. I hadn't seen the advertisement.

"It's our campaign for the new line," Conor replied. "Here, let me show you." He pulled out his phone, swiping until he found what he was looking for, then handed it to me. I stared at the picture. It showed a model with her back turned to the camera. All you could see was her bare shoulders and long blonde hair, and scattered through the strands were lilies, roses and wildflowers.

For the briefest second I thought, *she looks like me*.

But that was probably just my ego playing tricks.

It had to be a coincidence.

I handed the phone to Conor, glancing at Dylan when I said, "It's stunning."

His expression was guarded as he studied me for a reaction. I kept my face blank and was relieved when a waitress came and took our food orders.

The mood lightened after that. The four of us ate, drank, shared jokes, and talked about the old days. It was comforting, sort of like visiting with family even though we weren't. And I didn't fail to notice the way Conor looked at Yvonne.

And my aunt was as oblivious as ever.

"This is fun. Are you having fun?" she asked as we paid a visit to the ladies'. Her blue eyes shone with a merry gleam, a result of two pints of beer. She was such a lightweight.

I, on the other hand, was pacing myself. I didn't trust what I'd do to Dylan if I got too tipsy.

"I'm having lots of fun. So is Conor," I replied and stepped inside a stall.

"He's really grown up," she commented from the stall next to mine. "Like, I barely recognised him."

"Yep. And he's still got eyes for you."

She scoffed. "Oh, hush. He does not. I'm old enough to be his mother."

"If you got pregnant at *eight*. It's not that big of an age gap, Yvonne. Besides, I'm fairly sure you're not even old enough to be a cougar."

"Yes, well, I still think you're wrong. That boy is thirty years old, gorgeous, and probably earns six figures a year. Whereas I'm thirty-nine, earn a moderate wage, and well past my prime. I'm pretty sure he could do better."

"First of all, Conor is about as much of a boy as you are a girl. And second of all, don't you dare. You're gorgeous and smart and kind. If he can do better, I'll eat my hat."

"You're not wearing a hat."

"You're tipsy. Shut up."

We both emerged from our stalls and went to wash our hands. I caught Yvonne staring at me thoughtfully through the mirror and frowned. A moment ago, she'd been giddy, now she looked a little sad.

"What's wrong?"

She shook her head and glanced away. "I was just thinking, if Sam were here he'd have loved tonight."

My heart gave a hard thump. "He did love a good night out."

"I miss him," she whispered.

"Me, too."

We both focused on washing our hands before Yvonne spoke, changing the subject. "Anyway, please tell me you've noticed how Dylan's been looking at you all night. The man is besotted."

I frowned as I pumped some soap from the dispenser. "He said he wants to date me."

"Awww. That's so sweet. What did you say?"

I pursed my lips. "I told him I'm not ready."

Yvonne was quiet a moment, obviously thinking hard about something. "Can I be frank?"

"Only if I can be Susan."

She laughed and swiped me on the arm. "Be serious, Ev. I think after all these years you two deserve a second chance. The only time I've ever witnessed real love was you two as teenagers. It was clear how much you meant to each other."

Her words and kind sentiment formed a knot in my throat, and I suddenly felt very emotional. She was right. It had been true love, and if things had been different we might've been blissfully happy together.

It was difficult to say yes to trying again, especially when I couldn't stop thinking about all the years we'd lost.

But maybe I should. If we really were meant to be, it'd be a worse tragedy to waste any more time. I walked out of the bathroom in a tailspin. Dylan and Conor were still sitting in the booth, chatting casually. When Dylan looked up, a smile on his face that was all for me, my heart caught in my throat.

Over by the stage, people were dancing jigs to the live music.

"We should join them," Conor said, standing and offering his arm to Yvonne. She took it, and he led her to the dance floor. I stood in front of Dylan and his smile grew fonder.

"I guess you want to dance, too."

I grinned. "Oh, go on. You've twisted my arm."

Dylan shook his head and led me over. He held me close as the music thumped around us. It was traditional, with a punk edge. A flash of Yvonne's red dress caught my eye, and I saw her and Conor laughing as they butchered a jig.

"Come here," Dylan whispered and pulled me closer.

His lips brushed along my cheek and I suppressed a tremble at the feather-light sensation. I fell against him, knees weak, and wrapped my arms around his shoulders.

"I missed you," he went on sadly. "For so long I've missed you."

I turned my head into his neck and pressed my lips to his skin. "I missed you, too."

I felt a shudder run through him, my name a rasp on his tongue. "*Evelyn.*"

He ran his hand from my shoulder, down my back to rest to just above my backside. We stayed like that for a while, not really dancing but holding each other while all around us people moved. I pulled away from him when Yvonne tapped me on the shoulder.

"Conor and I are going to get more drinks. You want anything?"

"Yeah, get me a vodka and Coke," I replied.

I definitely needed it.

One drink led to another, and another, and before I knew it I was drunk as a skunk. So much for staying level-headed. Dylan's hand rested on my thigh as the four of us took a taxi back to his and Conor's place. It was two in the morning, but none of us were ready to say goodnight.

We tumbled into the house, a messy, drunken riot. Conor fiddled with the sound system, and *Of Monsters and Men* "Little Talks" came on way too loud. He and Yvonne started dancing giddily, while I wandered into the kitchen to find some water. I grabbed a bottle from the fridge when Dylan came up and wrapped his arms around me from behind.

"Stay the night," he whispered low.

"I won't let Yvonne go home on her own."

I heard rather than saw his smirk. "I've a feeling she won't be sleeping in her own bed tonight."

I twisted in his arms, trying to formulate thoughts past a haze of vodka. "Dylan . . . you and me . . . we . . . aren't having sex."

"But we're so good at it," he whined charmingly and tickled my hips. I laughed and struggled out of his hold. I made sure there was at least a foot of space between us when I pointed my finger at him.

"I'm serious. It's way too soon."

His smile slowly transformed into a look of passion. "You've been mine since the beginning of time, Ev. It's never too soon."

"We weren't around at the beginning of time," I argued and stumbled away from the fridge. I wandered into the living room and fell onto the couch. I lay there, staring at Yvonne and Conor acting silly when Dylan appeared in front of me.

He sat down and pulled the water bottle from my grasp. He took a swig then muttered quietly, "Feels like we were."

"Don't think you can charm me with your romantic ways, O'Dea, because I'm wise to it."

He chuckled and dropped his head to rest on my shoulder. "Oh Ev, you know me too well."

He joined me in watching Conor and Yvonne. "I think it'd make me happy if they got together," he said after a few quiet moments.

"Everybody loves a good caterpillar to butterfly story," I replied.

"Stop. Now I'm just picturing Conor's face on a butterfly," Dylan chuckled, and for some reason I thought it was the funniest thing ever. Obviously, my drunk self had a very basic sense of humour.

"What are you two laughing at?" Conor asked as he and Yvonne came to join us.

"You're such a pretty butterfly, Conor," I said and his brows furrowed.

"If you say so."

"He's more like a panther, a sexy panther," Yvonne blurted, and I knew she'd be embarrassed when she remembered saying that in the morning.

He shot her a flirty look. "If I'm a panther, you're a fox."

"Rawrrr," she growled. "Hold on, what sound does a fox make?" She was officially suffering from 'too much alcohol and dancing with a younger man all night' syndrome.

"Okay, I think it's bedtime," Dylan announced, standing from the couch. "Ev, you can stay in my room. Conor, Yvonne's staying with you, right?"

Conor opened his mouth to answer in what I suspected was a resounding yes, when my aunt butted in. "What? No. No way. This house is huge, there must be spare bedrooms." Maybe she wasn't as drunk as I thought.

"There are," Dylan said, "but they aren't made up."

"You can have my bed, and I'll sleep on the couch," Conor offered kindly.

She waved him away. "No, I couldn't possibly—"

"It's no trouble, I mean it."

Okay, someone needed to take control of this situation. "I tell you what. Why don't Yvonne and I sleep in Dylan's room, and Dylan, you can bunk up with Conor for the night. That way everybody gets a bed."

Dylan grabbed my hand, pulling me close. There was warning in his tone. "Evelyn."

"I think that's a great idea," Yvonne said, happy now.

Dylan let out the surrendering sigh of a man who knew he wasn't getting laid. "I'll go grab you both some T-shirts to sleep in."

"I'll get one for Yvonne, Dylan," Conor was quick to offer. *God.* No doubt he wanted that visual to last. Yvonne in one of his shirts.

Dylan cast him an arched look but didn't argue. He tugged on my hand and led me upstairs to his room, where he pulled two T-shirts out of the dresser. I plucked one from his hold, recognising it instantly. "Oh my God, I remember this." It was the exact same dark green Oasis T-shirt he'd worn when we were teenagers. "I can't believe you still have it."

Without thinking, I pulled my blouse up over my head and replaced it with the T-shirt. The room went so quiet you could hear a pin drop. I glanced at Dylan and his gaze darkened. He'd obviously caught a glimpse of my bra.

"Your boobs have gotten bigger," he commented.

I arched a brow as I tried not to blush. "They have not."

"Yes, they have. Want me to prove it?"

"Not if proving it involves you copping yourself a feel," I said, narrowing my gaze in playful suspicion. *I really, really wanted him to cop a feel.*

"Damn, foiled at the first hurdle."

I laughed, shucked off my jeans and climbed onto the bed. His navy duvet set felt cool and soft, probably Egyptian cotton. I laid my head against the pillow and closed my eyes. I was so tired, and the alcohol pulled me under.

I snapped alert and opened my eyes when I heard the slow scrape of Dylan's hand run across his stubble. He stared at me like I was a very tempting slice of chocolate cake.

Unconsciously, I wet my lower lip with my tongue.

"Fuck it," he swore and a second later he was on me. Before I had time to react, his mouth met mine, and my brains cells shut off. He cupped my jaw, and kissed me deeply with tongue. I wrapped my legs around his waist and his erection pressed between my thighs. I huffed a needy whimper and pulled him closer. He kissed me like he was already inside me. I clawed and pulled at his shirt buttons, needing them open. It was the sweetest relief when I finally got his chest bare and ran my hands down his smooth, hard abs. He might not have been a fan of the gym like Conor, but his body was absolutely one of my favourite things.

I'd never tire exploring the pathways of his skin.

"Oh, God. Sorry," came Yvonne's voice.

I pulled my mouth from Dylan's. My aunt stood in the doorway, hand covering her eyes. I'd find it adorable if I wasn't feeling so cock-blocked. Or well, vagina-blocked I guess. I dropped my head onto the pillow and burst out laughing.

"Go to sleep, you're drunk," Dylan whispered in my ear before he climbed off the bed. I noticed Yvonne wore a grey T-shirt Conor must've given her, but I didn't comment on it.

Dylan shot me one last hot look, a look that said *next time,* then closed the door behind him. I sighed and got up to use the bathroom. I splashed water over my face, having sweated off most of my make-up from earlier, and gargled with some of Dylan's mouthwash. I needed to get his taste out of my mouth, erase it from lips. I felt so aroused, so hot and bothered. I definitely wouldn't sleep with his kiss flavouring my lips. There wasn't much I could do about his smell though. This was his room, and it was everywhere. It was just as much a comfort as it was torture.

And I wondered, if my aunt hadn't interrupted us, would we have gone all the way?

If a fumble and a kiss with Dylan felt heavenly tonight, then having sex with him would be celestial. I wasn't sure I was equipped to deal with celestial right now, not when I was trying hard not to fall for him again. Maybe it was for the best that we were interrupted.

"Well," said Yvonne, up on her high horse. She stood by the door to the en-suite, arms folded.

I cast her a glance as I dried my face with a towel. "Well, yourself."

"Oh, no, no. I'm the one *welling* right now, Evelyn," she said, grinning happily as she pulled her dress over her head. "It's happening."

"What's happening?"

"You and Dylan, finding your way back to one another. I knew it would."

"What about you and Conor? All over each other like two big, horny potatoes."

She pointed a finger at me and walked into the bedroom. "First of all, that's not even a saying, and second of all . . . okay, I don't have a second of all, but you can shut your face."

"You liiiike him," I crooned.

She threw a pillow at my head then went to climb under the covers. "I already told you, he's too young."

"It's a modern world. Nobody cares about age gaps anymore."

"Oh, I beg to differ. People say they don't care, but really, they do. They talk behind your back. It's just one of those things."

"Well, I think you're wrong, and I bet Conor does, too."

She made a harrumph and plumped the pillow under my head. "We'll see."

"Yes, we will," I replied and reached over to turn off the lamp. Not ten seconds later, Yvonne started snoring. I grabbed the spare pillow to drown her out, and soon enough I was asleep, too.

Eight

I woke up to the smell of coffee.

My eyes were still closed as I spread my palms out on the sheets. This bed was so comfortable . . . and then it hit me.

Dylan.

Yvonne snored lightly next to me, but all I could see was her hair. Sitting up, I ran my hands through my own hair, fingers catching in the knots. Ugh. Last night we'd all gone *way* overboard. I was surprised I actually had the wherewithal not to sleep with Dylan.

The bedroom door was ajar, and I could hear him and Conor chatting in the kitchen. He had to have come in to leave the coffee. I'd probably had my mouth hanging open, snoring and drooling on the pillow. I picked it up and took a sip.

Nice. It was still warm.

I took a few more sips then crawled out of bed and quickly pulled on my jeans. I slipped into the bathroom to pee then wandered downstairs to the kitchen. Dylan and Conor sat by the counter drinking tea and eating marmalade on toast. It made me smile, because it was the type of thing we ate for breakfast in the old days.

Some things didn't change.

"Morning, blondie," Dylan said, his expression fond.

"Hey. Um, thanks for the coffee."

"No worries. Come sit. Do you want some toast?" he asked, gesturing to a stool.

"I'd love some."

"How's the head?" Conor asked, grinning.

"Not as bad as it should be," I replied then winced. "Did I call you a pretty butterfly last night, or is it just my imagination?"

Dylan laughed. "It's not your imagination. You definitely called him that."

I shot Conor an apologetic look. "Sorry."

He shrugged. "There are worse things to be called."

"Here." Dylan set a cup of tea in front of me.

"Thanks," I murmured and took a sip.

We chatted for a couple minutes, yet all the while I couldn't stop thinking about Dylan lying on me when I got into bed last night. If we hadn't been interrupted, things would've gone further.

Before long, Yvonne came downstairs. She'd changed back into her red dress, but she'd obviously paid a visit to the bathroom to freshen up and remove last night's make-up. She actually looked pretty fresh-faced all things considered, but I could tell from her expression she felt awkward.

"Morning everyone," she said, her voice scratchy. The hazards from shouting to make conversation in the bar last night.

"Yvonne. Let me make you something to eat," Conor offered, standing from his stool but she waved him off.

"No, no, I need to get home and shower. I have work in a little while."

118

He seemed disappointed. "Okay, well, I'll call you a taxi then."

"We can catch one on the street. Are you ready to go, Ev?"

I sensed her urgency and quickly nodded, wiping the toast crumbs from my hands. "Sure, just let me grab my bag."

I hurried to gather my things, then returned to the kitchen to say goodbye. Feeling brave, I approached Dylan, went up on my tiptoes, and gave him a peck on the cheek. "Thanks for last night. I had a great time," I murmured.

"My pleasure," he whispered and turned his head to catch my lips in a sneaky kiss. I pulled back, trying to scowl, but only succeeded in a crooked smile. He was so cheeky. And my insides felt all sorts of mushy and excited because of it.

"See you, ladies," Conor called as Yvonne hustled me out the door.

We were in a taxi before either one of us said anything, but then we both spoke at the same time.

"Why are you being so awkward?"

"I can't believe we stayed the night."

"It's not like we did anything." She was completely overreacting.

"Yes, well, it's not like me. I don't do that sort of thing."

"Why don't you? We had fun. You deserve to have fun, Yvonne."

"Then why do I feel so embarrassed?"

119

"Because you're overthinking it. Are you embarrassed because you danced with Conor?"

"Yes. He's so much younger than me, and well, look at him. He's gorgeous."

"As are you. He's actually liked you since forever. Maybe you need to enjoy his attention. I think he'd like the chance to woo you."

"I don't want to be wooed."

"Too bad. It's happening. I wouldn't be surprised if you hear from him again very soon."

She shook her head at me, flustered, and turned her attention out the window. Personally, I was eager to see how things transpired between them. Once Yvonne got over her hang-ups, they could be amazing together. Not to mention Conor wanted to buy a place here in New York. It was perfect timing for the both of them.

The next day I received an email from Dylan. He really seemed to enjoy this method of communication.

Monday 12:19 dylanod@dylanscents.com to evflynn21@gmail.com

Think I might warm a seat at the bar tonight. Are you working?

Monday 12:20 evflynn21@gmail.com to dylanod@dylanscents.com

Yessir.

Monday 12:22 dylanod@dylanscents.com to evflynn21@gmail.com

In that case, keep an eye out for the handsome geezer in a suit trying to get your attention. He's a real catch.

Monday 12:25 evflynn21@gmail.com to dylanod@dylanscents.com

Hmm, are you sure he isn't trying to sell me a timeshare? Because I'm not interested ;-)

Monday 12:26 dylanod@dylanscents.com to evflynn21@gmail.com

Is timeshare a euphemism? The winky face is confusing me.

Monday 12:27 evflynn21@gmail.com to dylanod@dylanscents.com

No. Get back to work ;-)

Monday 12:29 dylanod@dylanscents.com to evflynn21@gmail.com

Ah! Quit that. It's creepy.

Monday 12:31 evflynn21@gmail.com to dylanod@dylanscents.com

Do you have a fear of winky emojis? Because if you do I don't think we can date. I don't want to pass the affliction onto our offspring.

P.S. ;-) ;-) ;-)

Monday 12:34 dylanod@dylanscents.com to evflynn21@gmail.com

Don't worry. Winkiphobia skips a generation.

P.S. Stop it.

P.P.S. I thought dating was off the table??

Monday 12:36 evflynn21@gmail.com to dylanod@dylanscents.com

Phew! Good to know.

P.S. Winkiphobia sounds like a fear of small penises. FYI.

P.P.S. It is off the table, but it might be sitting in the pantry, waiting to be plucked off the shelf in time.

Monday 12:37 dylanod@dylanscents.com to evflynn21@gmail.com

God, I love you.

Going back to work now.

P.S. I'll live in hope. xxx

I stared at the screen for several minutes, fixating on those three little words. I mean, it shouldn't have been so shocking. We said the same thing to one another on a daily basis when we were kids. We were older now, but I still felt excited and fluttery like it was the very first time. Questions filled my head, like, was it just a force of habit? A slip of the tongue? Or *the type*, to be more exact. Did he mean he loved me romantically, or he loved talking to me, or was it simply that he'd always loved me? Or was it something he said now?

Gah, I was going to drive myself mad thinking in circles.

That night, a few hours into my shift, Dylan appeared. It was Monday, so the vibe in the bar was mellow. I was stacking some glasses when he took a seat in front of me. His hair was mussed and his tie loose. In all honesty, he looked tired but still happy to see me.

"Long day?"

He sighed. "The longest. Can I get a pint?"

"Sure. Anything you want to talk about?"

"Nothing very interesting. There's just a lot left to do to get the store fully functional, and I've been . . .

distracted," he said, eyeing me as he fiddled with a coaster. I took that to mean *I* was the distraction.

"You just need to sleep more. Sleep is life's miracle cure. You can face anything once you've had enough."

His eyebrow moved ever so slightly. "I'd sleep much better with someone beside me."

"I'm sure Laura would be happy to volunteer," I replied and regretted it when he frowned.

"Don't do that, Ev."

"Do what?"

"Muddy up what's happening between us," he said, gesturing me closer. I leaned a little over the bar and his voice lowered to a pitch I felt all the way between my thighs. "It feels natural, doesn't it?"

I couldn't say no, because it did. Dylan's return into my life was obliterating my usual negative thoughts. How could I feel depressed when he smiled at me like I hung the moon and stars?

I didn't answer him, but he probably saw agreement in my eyes. I went to pull his pint, and caught him studying me when I glanced his way.

"What?"

He wore a smile like he had a secret. "Just thinking."

"About?"

"Where I'm going to take you on our first date."

I narrowed my gaze, unable to help the smile playing on my lips. "Oh yeah? Well, you're looking at an eligible lady right here, so it better be good."

Dylan rubbed at his stubble, mischief glittering in his eyes. "I was thinking Burger King followed by a fumble in the bushes?"

I chuckled. He was being ridiculous, but I was charmed and played along. "I like it. Tell me more."

"We'll argue with the server that they didn't give us enough fries, then plant a hair in our burgers so we can get our money back."

"Damn, you know how to treat a girl."

"They should name me bachelor of the year."

"Definitely."

I chewed on my lip before I spoke again. "Speaking of bachelors, I'd love to hear about your past relationships. After all, I've told you all about mine."

My mind went back to our brief reunion eight years ago, when I left him that note. I'd encouraged him to go out and find love, but even now it hurt just to think about him with another woman. *Other women.*

He grimaced. "How about I don't?"

"Quid pro quo, my friend."

Dylan blew out a breath. I could tell he really didn't want to talk about this, but I was too curious to let him off the hook.

"My longest relationship was in San Francisco," he said finally.

"Ah, so that's why it's your favourite city," I replied, and tried to hide my pang of jealousy.

"That's not the reason," Dylan said. "It's my favourite place because I like the atmosphere and the people. Aside from LA, I was there the longest, so it makes sense that my longest relationship would be there, too."

"So, why did it end with San Fran girl?"

"She said I worked too much."

I arched a brow. "That's all?"

Dylan slid his teeth across his lower lip. "She also said I should've proposed to her on our one-year anniversary, but we were together a year and a half and there was no ring, so . . ."

"She cut you loose."

"Pretty much."

I wanted to ask if he'd loved her, but I wasn't *that* brave. Some part of me wanted to be the only one he'd truly ever loved, which was selfish, but I couldn't help it. Eleven years was a long time not to love anyone. Believe me, I knew.

Clearing my throat, I continued, "Anyone else?"

"Well, there was Anna in LA, and Veronica in Chicago, but those only lasted a couple months."

"And Laura in New York. You should write an R&B song," I mused.

Dylan chuckled softly before his expression sobered. He must've sensed some insecurity in me when he said, "Laura and I didn't date, Ev. Whatever it was is well and truly over. You know that, right?"

I stared at him a moment, but before I could respond a voice said, "Hey! You never called."

I blinked my attention away from Dylan to the person who spoke. It was a guy in a suit, and it took me a second to recognise him as the man who hit on me here at the bar a couple weeks ago. He'd complimented my accent and given me his business card.

I mustered a polite smile. "Hi, uh, can I get you anything?"

"You can get me your number, babe. I guarantee I'll use it."

Dylan frowned and cocked his head, all *is this arsehole for real?*

"Oh, well, that's against the management rules, I'm afraid. But I *can* get you a drink."

"Playing hard to get. I like it," he said, completely oblivious to Dylan's hard stare. "I'll take a gin and tonic, gorgeous."

I made his drink and handed it over. He placed a twenty on the bar, and I took it to the till before bringing back his change. As I slid the money towards him, he placed his hand over mine, leaning closer when he said, "If you give me your number, I promise I'll make it worth your while."

Dylan rose out of his seat and cleared his throat harshly. "I'll advise you to take your hand off my girlfriend."

The guy turned, looked at Dylan, then lifted his hand. "Hey, sorry, buddy. I didn't know the lovely lady here was taken."

He grabbed his drink off the bar, turned, and walked away. Obviously, flirting with me wasn't worth getting into a fight over. I placed more napkins and straws in the dispenser and glanced at Dylan. "Feel better now?"

He narrowed his gaze; my amusement clearly bothered him. "He touched you."

"This is a bar. Handsy types come with the territory. I'm well used to fending them off."

Dylan knocked back a gulp of his beer. "You shouldn't have to fend anyone off."

I nodded, because he was right. Still, the fact he referred to me as his girlfriend had my stomach in flutters. It was a lie to get the guy to leave, I knew that, but the way he said, all possessive, made something in me wake up and take notice. Besides, I understood how it felt to be jealous. Just thinking of him and Laura together made me want to grit my teeth.

Speaking of which, I needed to move past my issues about her. He said they were over, but I had to know if that was one hundred per cent true. I wanted to eventually get to a place where I was ready to date Dylan, and if I ever got there I had to get over him being around a woman he'd slept with. She worked for him, and no matter what went on between them, I'd never ask him to fire her and hire someone else. It wasn't my style.

"Can I ask you something?" I said. Dylan, whose attention had been fixed on his beer, lifted his eyes to mine.

"Ask me anything."

I chewed on my lip. "It's sort of related to what we were talking about earlier. About your exes."

He groaned, which was a little bit adorable. "Go on, then."

I steeled myself. "Well, it's kind of silly, but it's something that's been niggling at me. I know you said you and Laura were over, but why did she feel she could text you at four in the morning? Has she texted you since that night? Will she text you for a booty call again in the middle of the night?" I hated feeling so insecure—hated *sounding* insecure—but this was warranted. He must have been able to see that Laura wanted him, but I needed to know that he didn't feel the same.

He stared at me for a second, looking overwhelmed. "That's a lot of questions."

"Bit of an onslaught, I know. Sorry."

He scratched his jaw. "Don't be sorry. You have a right to know, and I have no problem being up front with you. To be honest, I have no clue why she texted me at four in the bloody morning. In fact, it pissed me off. Mostly because it interrupted my time with you."

I swallowed then nodded. He continued speaking. "I told her it was inappropriate, which I know is a bit of a double standard, but it was the only way I could think to set her straight. She hasn't done it again since, so she got the message."

He paused then reached across the bar to take my hand in his. "I haven't wanted anyone else. I feel like I've been waiting for you, if you want the truth. Yes, there were other women, and I think I dated and stayed awhile with some of them because it was better than being alone in some ways. You . . . you said you wanted me to find someone in your note."

I blinked and looked away. "I did."

128

He squeezed my hand. "And I tried to, believe me, I tried. But none of them, *none of them* hold a candle to you, Ev."

He took a deep breath and held my hand to his heart. "It's always only been you. It only ever will be."

Nine

"Ev, you can head home now. Your shift's over," said Ger, the other bartender on duty.

I blinked several times and turned to him. "Right. Thanks."

He frowned. "Are you okay?"

"Perfectly fine," I said and stepped by him. Dylan sat at the bar. His eyes followed me as I went into the staffroom to collect my things. His voice echoed in my head, his romantic words warming all the parts of me that were cold. The way he looked at me was all-consuming. Most people could only dream of being looked at in such a way. And there he was right in front of me, his eyes telling me I could have him if only I was brave enough to reach out and take.

He made me weak. He made me *want*. Every part of me fizzled with the need to feel his touch, to touch him in return. It was so much I could hardly stand it any longer.

I walked out, and he was still there. His eyes asked a question. I came closer, swallowing several times as I gathered my nerve, then said, "Take me home."

Dylan didn't breathe a word, only nodded and stood to offer me his hand. We didn't have too much trouble hailing a taxi, but it was a quiet journey. Pent-up emotions clogged the enclosed space.

"You left your top at my apartment," Dylan said, stroking a hand through my hair.

"I know," I replied, not looking at him. "And I still have your T-shirt."

"Keep it," he offered and I smiled.

"I did always love it on you."

The taxi stopped then, and Dylan paid the driver. He got out first and came around to open my side. I didn't know what I was doing bringing him home with me, but after our conversation at the bar, I wasn't ready to say goodnight.

When it came to Dylan, I'd never been ready to say goodnight.

I couldn't believe how quickly I'd fallen back under his spell. Sure, in the time we'd been apart I'd thought about him almost every day, but that didn't mean I ever expected to see him again. Especially not after that night we spent together in his tiny, cheap hotel room. I fled before he woke up, and left nothing but a hasty, sentimental note written on the back of an envelope.

I led him upstairs to the apartment, placing my finger to my lips for him to be quiet. "Yvonne's asleep," I said and slotted my key in the door.

We stepped inside, and Dylan silently helped me off with my coat. His eyes traced my features, focusing on my lips. I turned and dropped my keys into the bowl on the coffee table.

"Want some tea?" I whispered.

"Sure," he replied and took a seat on the couch.

"Okay, I'll be right back," I said, going to turn the electric heater on in my bedroom. The building didn't have a great boiler, so my room was really cold some nights. I was almost to my door when two arms wrapped around me from behind. I shuddered when he dipped his mouth to my neck and gave a kiss.

"I don't really want tea," he murmured.

"What do you want?" I asked shakily.

"You," he replied, then walked me forward until my chest met the wall. He held me there, captive. His erection pushed into my lower back, while his mouth licked and sucked at my neck. I was so aroused I couldn't think straight.

"Be with me tonight," he whispered, hand groping down the front of my body, over my breasts and stomach before dipping between my legs. I arched my back when he cupped me there, and a low rumble emanated from deep in his chest.

His hand gripped the back of my neck and he directed me toward my bedroom. Without the heater on, I knew it must've been freezing, but I couldn't feel the cold. I was too busy burning from Dylan's touch. Still behind me, he carefully lowered me onto the bed. He reached around my body to massage my breast over the top of my clothes, then lowered his hands to undo my pants. In an abrupt movement he yanked them down, revealing my knickers. He ran his hands over the lace then pulled those down, too.

Seconds later his mouth was on me, and I gasped at the sensation.

Dylan O'Dea, perfumer and businessman extraordinaire, was eating me out from behind.

My mouth gaped as I panted. I wanted to moan but I had to stay quiet in case Yvonne heard. I made a small yelp when his teeth grazed my clit, and he clucked his tongue.

"Not a sound, Evelyn. We can't be heard," he chided naughtily. I squeezed my eyes shut and clenched my teeth. His mouth felt way too good for silence.

"This is torture," I whispered.

"The good kind, I hope," Dylan teased and pulled my legs farther apart to get a better angle. I gasped. "God, I've missed you. Your taste. Your body." He pushed me higher and higher until I couldn't hold back anymore.

I came with a shudder and had to bite down on my pillow to keep from screaming. Dylan quickly flipped me on my back and pulled my top up over my head. He did away with my bra and pulled his own shirt off, too. I helped him with his trousers, but his blasted belt was being difficult.

He laughed huskily at my frustration and I finally managed to get it open.

"Eager," he whispered then caught my mouth in a deep, erotic kiss. We stayed like that for a while. I was less frantic now that I'd come, and I wanted to savour him. Dylan's cock pressed against my inner thigh and the hot, hard feel of it sent my hormones into a tailspin. My arousal built again, and still kissing him, I reached out to open my bedside table. I fumbled blindly through the bits and pieces until my fingers met the smooth, cool foil I was searching for.

Dylan broke our kiss. "What on earth are you—?"

He stopped when I held up the condom then smirked. "Prepared, are we?"

I grinned. "I was saving it for a special occasion."

He plucked it from my grasp and tossed it aside. "Were you now?" he murmured, capturing my mouth in his. I got lost in his lips again, and when he slid inside me for a second, I gasped. He grunted and pulled out, feeling around the bed for the condom.

"Better put this on," he said gruffly.

I watched in horny fascination as he slid the rubber down his length then came closer. He held himself above me, gazed down at me, and breathed, "My muse."

He didn't take his eyes off me when he pushed inside, and his entire body shuddered in pleasure.

He made love to me slowly. With every inhale he took, I exhaled. For every inhale I took, he exhaled. Both of us were conscious to avoid making any sound, but somehow that made everything more intense.

Grey light filtered through the window. It was late. So late it was almost early.

Dylan and I made love until the sun started to move above the horizon, the golden rays filtering through the deep blue depths of his irises. We fell asleep, and with his entire body curled around me, it was the most peaceful I'd felt in over a decade.

Ten

"Morning," Dylan whispered huskily in my ear. My body felt sore but languid, an after effect of the amazing things we'd done last night.

All. The. Things. We'd. Done.

What on earth had possessed me?

Oh right. Now I remembered. Dylan worked his romantic charms, and I simply couldn't keep my knickers on. He sucked and nuzzled my neck as he pressed his thickening erection into the curve of my lower back. I moaned when his hand dipped between my legs. I was wet already.

His skilled fingers slid down my folds and dipped inside for a second. I arched my spine in invitation for him to keep going.

"I could stay here all day making you come," he murmured just as I heard movement out in the kitchen. There was the recognisable clink of Yvonne placing her breakfast dishes in the sink. I froze and wondered if she heard my moan. Embarrassment seized my body. I mean, she'd never expect things to progress as quickly with Dylan as they had. She probably thought . . . man, she probably thought I was making use of the vibrator that was buried under a pile of T-shirts at the bottom of my wardrobe.

Not that she knew I had it or anything.

"What's wrong?" Dylan asked, and I scrambled to cover his mouth.

"Yvonne's out there," I whispered, and his lips formed a smirk behind my hand.

"You're not a teenager anymore, Ev. You're allowed to have sex."

"Yes, I know that. I'm just . . . embarrassed, okay?"

His gaze softened, and I resented how handsome he looked when he did that. "You're fucking adorable."

I scowled but didn't say anything, waiting for Yvonne to leave for work. Glancing at the clock, it was almost eight. She always left the apartment at eight on the dot. I knew because I usually woke up to the slam of the door being shut then would drift back off to sleep until midday.

Regular as clockwork, the door opened and closed with a loud snick. I slumped back into the pillows in relief.

Dylan stroked my hair away from my forehead, staring down at me with affection. "I should be leaving, too," he said with regret.

I swallowed. "Listen, Dylan, about last night—"

His finger went to my lips to stop me. "Let's just enjoy this, Ev. I know you're still not ready, and I'm willing to be patient. We can go at whatever pace you need."

God, he was too perfect.

I let out a low chuckle. "We just spent the night having sex. Pretty sure my pace is completely out of whack."

"Well then, for now we can be friends. Really, *really* close friends," he said, with a devilish grin.

136

I shoved him away and rolled my eyes, even though the idea of being friends with Dylan while being able to use his body for sex was dead appealing. I felt like a bit of a scumbag for thinking it, but there it was.

"I've been meaning to ask you," he went on, distracting me from my thoughts. "I have a charity event I'm attending tomorrow night, and I'd love if you'd be my date. It's to raise money for homelessness."

"Oh," I said, taken off guard. "I mean, I'd love to go but I have nothing to wear to something like that."

"Evelyn, when are you going to realise that I couldn't care less what you're wearing? You own a dress, don't you?"

"Well, yes, but—"

"Then that's perfect. I'll pick you up at eight."

Before I had a chance to respond, he was out of bed and pulling on the clothes he'd shed last night. I admired his naked form before it was covered, then got up, and headed into the kitchen.

"Do you want breakfast before you go?" I called back.

He came out of my room, sliding his tie around his neck. "I'm in a real hurry, love. But maybe next time."

"That's okay," I said and went to put some toast on for myself. My thighs clenched at the idea of a next time. Dylan wrapped his arms around me from behind and pressed his lips to my neck. "I'll miss you today."

"Me, too," I whispered in reply.

He caught my mouth in a quick kiss then hustled to the door, turning back just before he left. "See you tomorrow, Evelyn."

***

Later that day evening, about an hour before I had to go to work, my inbox pinged with a new email.

Tuesday   17:11   dylanod@dylanscents.com   to evflynn21@gmail.com

I've been thinking about you all day . . .

Tuesday   17:13   evflynn21@gmail.com   to dylanod@dylanscents.com

Me, too.

About you, I mean.

Tuesday   17:15   dylanod@dylanscents.com   to evflynn21@gmail.com

Can I call you?

I chewed on my lip, wondering what he wanted to talk about, then shot off a simple reply: YES. My phone lit up with a call not long after.

"Hey," I answered, hesitant. Now that we had a day of distance between us, I felt unsure of myself. I also felt selfish for leading him on, especially when I didn't know how long it would take for me to be ready for a proper relationship.

I was officially one of those indecisive arseholes who strung people along.

Oh God . . .

I was Kourtney Kardashian.

But then, that would mean Dylan was Scott, and he was absolutely *nothing* like him.

138

And yes, having no close friends and no social life these past few years left a lot of room for reality TV.

"Evelyn," he breathed. He sounded . . . aroused, and my stomach flipped at the mere idea of a turned-on Dylan.

"What did you want to talk about?" I asked tightly, trying to sound normal when I was feeling anything but.

"I can't stop thinking about last night . . ." A sigh. "The noises you made, your taste."

My breathing grew choppy, his voice working me up. I really hoped he was someplace private. "I've been thinking about it, too."

"Do you know how much I've missed the feel of you?" he went on. "All day I've wanted you in my arms."

I swallowed and closed my eyes. This was on the verge of turning into phone sex, and I was helpless to stop it.

"Where are you right now?"

"In my bedroom," I whispered. "Getting ready for work."

He swore under his breath. "I'm at the office."

"Mm-hmm."

"Come over. I want to fuck you on my desk."

"Dylan," I gasped. When we were younger, he'd never been shy, but this grown-up version of him was very forward. He didn't mince his words. *And a part of me liked that very much.*

"Come over," he repeated.

"I can't. I have a shift."

"You can call in sick," he argued, a seductive lilt to his voice.

I lay back on my bed and my hand somehow found its way to my stomach, my palm flat to my skin. "You'll see me tomorrow," I whispered.

He groaned softly. "I'm not sure I can wait that long."

"It'll be a lesson in delayed gratification," I said, teasing now.

He swore under his breath. "This entire day has been a lesson in delayed gratification."

The strained needfulness in his voice caused the spot between my thighs to ache. My hand moved lower. I slipped it under the hem of my knickers and between the folds of my sex. I was wet, so wet, and all from a small amount of time on the phone with Dylan. I must've made some sort of noise, because he emitted a low, rumbling groan.

"What are you doing?"

"Just keep talking."

"Fucking hell, Ev."

I circled my finger around my clit, my hips arching instinctively. My breathing grew heavy as I felt an orgasm build. Dylan had this magic that was all his own; he could make me come just from talking.

"Remember when I used to go down on you in your bedroom before school? I could taste you on my mouth all day afterwards," he said, and it drove me higher.

"And that time we made love in the storage cupboard at the back of the chemistry lab? It's still the best sex I've ever had."

"You pushed me up against the cupboard," I said past a moan, remembering. "I thought someone would walk in."

"But they didn't. You came while I was still inside you. It felt incredible."

"God . . . *Dylan* . . ."

"It was so hard to concentrate during lessons, when I knew you were just a few rooms away."

"You caught me between classes often enough," I said, panting.

"Couldn't help it. I'd spend half of my physics lab daydreaming about your body, how you felt when I was inside you. Some days . . . I just couldn't wait until school ended. And that first time you sucked my cock, Christ, Ev . . ."

"Oh, God, Dylan, I'm gonna . . ."

I was silent when my orgasm hit. It was swift and intense. I clenched my thighs, swallowing as it subsided.

"Jesus," he muttered down the line. "Do you know how hard I am right now?"

As soon as the pleasure petered out, I was filled with a sense of embarrassment, which was ridiculous given what we did last night.

"Dylan, I—"

"No. Don't you dare, Ev. There's no shyness between us, okay?"

My reply was a whisper, "Okay."

"You feel good?"

I flushed. "Yeah."

"Good. Maybe tomorrow you'll let me make you feel good in person."

I couldn't help my sigh. When we hung up I flopped back in bed, wondering how on earth I was going to get through an entire shift after having phone sex with Dylan, his husky, beguiling voice replaying my head.

The next day, I managed to convince Yvonne to lend me her red dress to wear to the charity event. I was a little bigger than she was, but it still fit me okay. The contoured design meant it clung to every curve. I understood why she was always so hesitant to wear it, because although it went to just below the knee, it still left very little to the imagination.

"Look at you," she crooned when I stepped out of my bedroom. "Jessica Rabbit."

I smirked and waved a hand at her. "Oh shush." Then conspiratorially. "But tell me more."

"You look gorgeous. Dylan's going to lose his mind. I can't believe you two are going on a date. I feel giddy."

"Well, you can set your giddy pants aside for now. Yes, I'm his date, but it's not *a date*."

Yvonne scrunched her brows. "That doesn't even make sense."

"It does in my head."

The door buzzed, so I grabbed my coat and bag. I didn't want Yvonne making any more of a song and dance, so I headed downstairs to meet Dylan instead of inviting him up. He stood in the lobby wearing a tux. A TUX. My libido just about ~~died~~ went to heaven.

RIP.

My long coat was buttoned all the way up. I wasn't ready to show him the dress yet, even though he'd already seen it on Yvonne. It was just so . . . boobsy. And while my aunt was a B-cup, I was a D. Two letters made a world of difference.

Dylan's brow arched slightly. He could tell I was hiding something. "What's up with you? Nervous?"

"It's boobsy," I blurted and he let out a confused laugh.

"Pardon?"

"My dress. It shows a lot of—"

"Décolletage?"

"Yes." Damn, that was a good word. Way better than boobsy.

His lips curved as he stepped closer. "Okay, now I have to see."

I held a hand out. "Not until we get to the event."

He reached for me and clasped my shoulders in his palms. "Why not now?"

I shot him an arch look. "Because if I do we won't make it to the event."

"No?"

I stepped by him and moved toward the door, where a town car idled just outside. "No. You'll get all handsy with my boobsys."

Dylan let out a bark of a laugh. "God, you're so weird."

His tone said *God, I adore you*, which was why a rosy blush coloured my cheeks. He stepped ahead of me and opened the door to the waiting car. I slid inside, feeling like an imposter but also loving the opulence. I was one of those people who were all, *spa days are for spoiled housewives*. But then as soon as someone said they're paying, I was already in a bathrobe, cucumber slices on each eye, while a lady dressed in white gave me a pedicure.

Even in Yvonne's lucky red dress, I still felt intimidated when we arrived at the hotel where the event was being held. With Dylan's hand in mine, I looked around, taking it all in. What was it about rich people that somehow made them look glossier than us regular folk?

Money, probably.

"It's all those face creams with the baby foreskin mixed in," Dylan replied, because yes, I'd asked the question out loud. I screwed up my mouth in disgust.

"Is that actually a thing?"

He shrugged. "Might be."

"Ugh. The saying is true that some people have more money than sense."

He chuckled low. "That they do."

"I'm a little nervous," I confessed.

Dylan came and caught my chin between his fingers, then laid a soft kiss on my lips. "Have I mentioned how beautiful you look tonight?"

"Maybe. But you can mention it again if you like."

"You're beautiful, Evelyn."

"Why, thank you," I said and linked my arm through his. "Now let's go get some food. I'm starved. They better have good appetizers at this thing."

"For twenty thousand a table I'm sure they do"

"Twenty K a table? Wow. Some people really do have more money than sense."

"It's for charity, Ev."

"Yeah, yeah," I said. "You all just like to swish around in fancy getups and feel like you're making the world a better place."

He cast me an amused look. "You're in a sassy mood tonight." He moved closer, his lips at my ear when he breathed. "Maybe later I'll fuck it out of you."

My breath got stuck in my throat, butterflies flitting around in my stomach. I swallowed and mustered a bold expression. "Will you now?"

He didn't answer, only smiled with confidence, took my hand and led me farther into the event. Pleasurable goose bumps danced along my neck.

A little while later, we were seated at a table. Dylan and I sat with a few other people from his company, including Conor. I was surprised he came without a date, then wondered if he'd asked Yvonne. That wagon better not have turned him down. I knew she wanted him, she just wouldn't allow herself to have him.

"That dress looks way better on your aunt," he commented as though reading my mind. I stuck out my tongue.

"Well, of course *you'd* think that."

Dylan chuckled and took a swig from his glass. "Don't listen to him. You look amazing."

"Hello, Mr O'Dea. Mr Abrahams."

All three of us turned to see Laura standing by our table. She wore a sparkly black dress that made her red hair appear particularly striking, her lips coated in a dark matte lipstick. The look was very femme fatale, and very geared towards impressing Dylan, I imagined. I couldn't help the way it made my gut tighten with envy. She looked incredible.

Her eyes wandered from Dylan and then to me, lingering a moment on the way his hand rested on my thigh. There was a brief flash of jealousy in her gaze and then it was gone.

"Laura, you look well," Conor said.

"Yes, good to see you," Dylan added stiffly.

After our conversation the other night, he knew I was wary of their past. I felt like he was being careful not to do or say anything that might make me suspect he still liked her. And that made me feel bad, because I didn't want him walking on eggshells.

"I really like your dress," I said kindly, hoping Dylan saw it as a sign that I didn't mind her being here. If they were over, there was no need for any weirdness. This thing between us was so new, there was no point being uptight.

She cast a glance my way. "Thanks. Yours is very . . . red."

Well, at least she didn't call it slutty. There wasn't really any response I could give, so I simply smiled politely and sipped my wine.

Laura took her seat on the other side of the table and chatted with some of her colleagues, but every once in a while, her eyes landed on me. Although she put on a good mask, I could see her displeasure. And I couldn't even blame her for hating me. If I'd had Dylan as a temporary bedfellow, I'd be dreaming up notions of more just the same as she was.

I made a mental note to talk to her later, clear the air somehow. If she was going to be working at *Dylan* for the foreseeable future, we needed to at least be civil.

My chance came when she headed for the bathrooms. I excused myself to Dylan and followed after her. She went inside a stall, but didn't notice me. I dawdled by the sink, and checked my appearance while I waited for her to emerge.

I felt odd waiting there, but this needed to be done. Other than her fondness for Dylan and dislike of me, she seemed like a decent person.

I pretended to wash my hands when she came out. She looked up, halting a moment when she saw me, then continued to the sink.

"Hi, Laura," I said, trying to sound friendly. "Are you having a good night?"

She narrowed her eyes ever so slightly. "Yes, I'm having a lovely night, Evelyn. Thank you for asking."

If I wasn't mistaken, her tone was a smidge tetchy.

"Well, I'm glad."

"And I'm glad that you're glad," she snipped, not bothering to hide her displeasure now.

I was above replying with, *I'm glad that you're glad that I'm glad.*

But just *barely.*

"Look, I want to clear the air."

She put a hand out to stop me. "Don't bother. I'm sure Dylan's told you all about us. He's not the type to hide that sort of thing, but if you think we're going to be friends you've got another think coming. I knew him for months and then you just came along, and poof, he's taking you out on dates and telling me not to call or text him anymore. Do you know how awful that feels?"

My guy clenched, because I suddenly felt bad for her. I tried to see things from her point of view and knew it must've hurt to be rejected like that. My expression was empathetic when I replied, "I'm sorry, you must feel horrible."

She sniffled and went to grab a tissue "Don't be nice. I don't need you turning out to be a kind person on top of all this."

What she said made me smile a little, because it was exactly what I might've said if I were in her position. Maybe Laura wasn't so bad . . .

"Please don't tell him I cried in here. I already cried in front of him when I screwed up an order at work the other week. I'm sure he thinks I'm an emotional and weak woman."

I arched a brow. "If he ever thought that I wouldn't be with him."

Wait, *was* I with him?

Laura groaned and crumpled up her tissue. "God, you are nice."

I shrugged. "I like to think I'm not a complete bitch. Dylan and I were childhood sweethearts," I said. "He came back into my life recently, and well, it's all been a little out our control really."

"Oh." She took a deep breath and nodded, and then I saw resolution in her expression.

She went over to the mirror to fix her make-up. "That makes more sense." I wasn't sure exactly what that meant, but for some reason it made her smile. *Did she think it was only because there was history between Dylan and me that he was interested in me now rather than her?*

"You don't have to explain. I'd rather hate you than like you, but I get it." *She gets what?*

After she'd touched up her lipstick, she let out a tired sigh. "Listen, I'm not stupid, I can see how Dylan looks at you. I know trying to get him back is pointless, and I love my job too much to jeopardise it that way. Still, I've barely known him six months and already I can tell he's one of the best and most talented men I've ever met. I hope you know how lucky you are."

She dropped her lipstick back in her bag then walked out the door. I didn't know what to make of her little speech, but it did make me question if I *was* good enough for Dylan. I still didn't understand why he had such high opinions of me. At least when we were teenagers, I'd been cheerful and full of life. I had passion. Now I was a directionless bartender who enjoyed watching mindless reality TV, painting her nails, and wasting time laughing at Internet memes in her spare time.

I wasn't special.

Not like Dylan.

As though my thoughts summoned him, he appeared outside the bathroom when I emerged. He took my hand, eyes bright like he was excited for some unknown reason.

"Come on, I want to show you something," he said, and I let him pull me down the hallway. We walked through the main function room and out into a smaller atrium. People stood drinking wine and eating canapés, but at the centre of the room was a large and very impressive flower display. It was similar to the one out front, only bigger and more intricate.

"One of the sponsors of the event owns a flower farm in New Jersey called Hillview. They made all of the arrangements."

"They're beautiful," I said, and I meant it. Looking at the display made my heart beat faster, like I could see a life for myself through fractured glass. One I could've had if things had been different. One I still could have if I was brave enough to take a chance.

The idea was more powerful now that I was becoming fixated on how ordinary I felt compared to Dylan.

The display was like an artistic expression of a meadow. There were forget-me-nots and pansies, gardens mums and morning glories. It was an explosion of colour to dazzle the eyes, a feast of scents to seduce your nose.

"I know the owner," Dylan said. "I buy flowers from him on occasion when I'm developing new perfumes."

"Oh?" I replied, curious.

"Would you like to meet him?"

I narrowed my gaze, both charmed and disgruntled at the same time. "You know I do, you bastard."

He chuckled. "I said I'd get you gardening again."

"Yes," I answered back. "And your determination knows no bounds."

His smile was everything as he turned and guided me back into the main function room.

Eleven

"Mr Harrington," Dylan greeted. "May I introduce you to my date, Evelyn Flynn?"

The older gentleman turned to us with a kind smile. "You can, of course, but be warned, I might have to steal her because she is ravishing."

"Hello, Mr Harrington," I said. "It's a pleasure to meet you. Your flower display is amazing."

"The pleasure is all mine, dear, and please call me Frank. My staff made the display. I'm just the old codger who pays their wages."

"Don't listen to him. He does a whole lot more than that," Dylan said.

"Oh well, please let them know they did an incredible job," I added.

"Evelyn here is a gardener, too," Dylan went on. "I used her flowers in my very first perfume."

Frank's eyes widened with interest. "Really? And where do you work now?"

My chest constricted at his question, and all of a sudden it was harder to breathe. I didn't expect to react this way. I also didn't expect the excitement that lay beneath the difficulty breathing. I was excited to talk to someone who owned a flower farm, someone who let his workers create beautiful displays with the things they grew.

But then, I felt unworthy, because I had no achievements of my own. No farm to boast about.

"Oh, I don't garden anymore," I said.

"I'm trying to convince her to start again," Dylan added. "But she's a stubborn one."

Frank's expression was amiable. "Well, if you ever want to dip a toe, I'd be happy to have you at my place. We always need extra pickers, though we're coming to the end of fall now, so things are quieter."

"That's very kind of you, but—"

"She'd love to," Dylan said, and I shot him an irritated glance.

Frank chuckled, obviously noting Dylan's enthusiasm and my apprehensiveness. "Why don't you *both* drop by this Saturday and I'll give you a tour?"

"We'll be there," Dylan replied and then Frank excused himself to mingle with other guests.

Dylan turned to beam at me. "Well, what do you think?"

"I think he's only being so welcoming because of his business relationship with you. I could be anyone."

"But that's the thing. You aren't just anyone, and once he gets to know you he'll see that."

"Hmm," I said, feeling like this whole evening had been a trap, even if it was a well-meaning, kind-hearted trap on Dylan's part.

He slid his hand affectionately down my arm. "Think about it. We don't have to go if you don't want to."

"Yeah, okay. I'm going to the bar."

I felt his eyes on my back as I walked away. Conor stood by the bar, sipping on a drink.

"Is that a Bellini?" I asked, amused by his choice.

"It's cheat day and I'm partial to fruity cocktails. So sue me."

"I didn't see you ordering any of those when we were out with Yvonne."

"That's because I need her to see me as a big, sexy manly man. I'll wait until the fourth or fifth date to reveal my girly preferences."

I chuckled. "Speaking of, did you invite her tonight?"

"I did. She said she was working."

That lying wench.

Conor grimaced. "I take it from your expression that was a lie."

"My aunt has issues."

He held out a hand. "Totally understandable given she knew me when I was a skinny little kid with acne and giant glasses."

"That shouldn't matter. I can tell she likes you. It's just, Yvonne's never excelled at relationships. I think she prefers the controllable predictability of being single. That way she doesn't have to worry about getting hurt."

Conor nodded, thoughtful for a moment. "Can you talk to her for me? Let her know I really, *really* like her. She can pretty much have me any way she wants me."

Well, that was interesting. It'd be sexy if he wasn't talking about my blood relative. I studied him speculatively. "What is it about my aunt that you like so much? I mean, you must have your pick of the ladies over here."

His lips curved in a smirk. "Is that a compliment?"

I poked him in the arm. "You know it's true."

He took a sip of his drink and shrugged. "I just really like her. She doesn't judge people, you know? Back home I was so used to everyone looking at me funny because of the colour of my skin. They'd do this little double take when I came around a corner. But Yvonne never did that, she just smiled and spoke to me like I was a normal person."

My chest ached a little at his explanation. "You *were* a normal person."

"I know that now, but it was hard to feel that way when I was younger."

I pursed my lips, remembering some of the mean, backhanded comments people would whisper about him. It wasn't outright bullying or racism, but I was sure it made Conor feel like crap sometimes. Like he didn't belong. And aside from his family, it wasn't like there was anyone else who could relate to his situation. Where we lived, everyone was white. Then Yvonne came along, full of sunshine and pretty smiles, and she treated him like any other person. I wasn't surprised she'd made a lasting impression.

I reached out and squeezed his arm. "I'll talk to her, okay?"

Conor shot me a grateful smile before Dylan appeared at my side. "Everything all right?"

I nodded, still a little put out by him foisting me on Frank Harrington like some sort of charity case who needed a job. I had a job. It just wasn't as fulfilling as Dylan thought flower farming would be. He was right, of course. I think it bothered me even more that he was right.

"Yes, fine," I said finally.

"Hey, do you two want to find a quiet bar somewhere for a few drinks? I'm not really feeling the stuffy atmosphere in here," Conor said and an idea sprung to mind. After our little heart to heart, I wanted to do something nice for him.

"I've got a better idea. Why don't we all go back to my place? I have some beers in the fridge."

"Are you sure Yvonne won't mind?" Conor asked warily.

I waved him away. "Not at all. Yvonne loves company." I knew she be annoyed at me for outing her lie to Conor that she was working tonight, but he already knew it was an excuse, so there was no point keeping up the charade.

Besides, if everything went to plan, she'd be thanking me for my determination to get them together before long.

***

I slotted my key in the door and led Conor and Dylan inside. The living room was empty, so I thought Yvonne must've gone to bed. I hoped she wasn't asleep yet.

"Make yourselves comfortable. I'm going to get out of this dress."

Dylan gave a sultry look. "I can help with that."

"Nice try. I'll be back in a minute."

I went into my room to change into my pyjamas, navy sweatpants and a *Wicked* T-shirt that read, 'Defy

Gravity'. Yvonne took me to see the show the week I arrived, and I bought the T-shirt from the merchandise stand, cracking a joke to the girl by asking if its witchy magic would ensure my boobs *defied gravity*. I told the same joke to Yvonne every time I wore it, but she stopped finding it funny after the fourth or fifth time.

I went to knock on her bedroom door, but when I didn't get an answer I ducked my head inside. She sat in bed reading a book, her hair in a knot, eyes wide.

"Who's out there?" she whispered.

I closed the door and stepped inside. "Just Conor and Dylan. We got bored at the gala and decided to come here. I hope that's okay."

"No, it isn't okay. Conor invited me tonight and I told him I was working. I'm going to have to hide in here until they leave."

"Yvonne, I'm pretty sure Conor knows that was a lie. He isn't stupid. He knows you don't want to date him."

She chewed on her lip, looking torn. "Do you think I should go out there and apologise?"

"I'm sure he'd appreciate your honesty."

She took a deep breath. "Okay, just let me fix my hair first." She went over to her dresser, pulled her hair out of its knot and ran a brush through it. "How do I look?"

"Gorgeous. Now come on. We have visitors waiting."

When we emerged, Dylan and Conor sat chatting on the couch. I went to grab the beers from the fridge while Yvonne approached Conor.

"Hey," she said, voice quiet. "I'm sorry for fobbing you off about tonight."

He gave her a soft look. "Don't worry about it."

"Can I give you a hug?"

His expression warmed. "Sure."

She approached him and threw her arms around his shoulders. He held on to her for a long moment, squeezing tight before he let go. I shared a look with Dylan. We both wanted something to happen between them, but we knew there was no point meddling. Well, not any more than I'd already meddled by bringing Conor to the apartment.

I set the beers on the coffee table and told everybody to take one. Yvonne declined, instead opting to make herself a cup of peppermint tea.

"Oh, Ev, you're wearing the T-shirt. Tell them your joke," she said as she came back in and settled down on an armchair.

I shot her a wry look. "I thought you hated that joke." Also, it wasn't so much a joke as a funny statement. At least, I found it funny, because I was a dork.

"I do, but that's only because I've heard it twenty times."

"What's the joke?" Dylan asked, gaze skimming the curve of my hip. I thought of our phone call last night and flushed all the way to my toes.

I took a swig of beer. "So, I got this T-shirt when Yvonne took me to see *Wicked*, and I asked the girl on the merch stand if it had magical powers, and if so, did it enable the wearer's boobs to *defy gravity*."

"That is one terrible, cheesy fucking joke," Conor chuckled.

"Yeah, I never knew your sense of humour could sink so low," Dylan added teasingly.

"Hey, I have a great sense of humour," I protested, smiling. I felt a little tipsy from the wine at the event and the beer I was currently drinking.

"If by great you mean an eighties sex comedy," he said, hoping to get a rise out of me. I could tell by the shine of mischief in his eyes. I wasn't going to let him win, trying to think of a snappy comeback.

"Well, you . . . *you* have the sense of humour of a politician making a joke about a rival politician, like *he's wants to fix the problems in education, but he can't even fix his own hair in the morning*, and then everyone in their party starts laughing like it's the funniest thing they've ever heard."

Dylan chuckled loudly. "That is quite possibly the most specific putdown I've ever heard."

"Didn't you ever watch Oireachtas TV back home? They're always cracking jokes like that," I said. "It's upsetting."

Yvonne laughed. "Upsetting?"

"Yes, anything that cringe-worthy is incredibly upsetting."

We spent the next hour chatting and drinking, and it all felt so effortless between the four of us. In fact, it was really nice, like a little slice of home. I'd been distracted by a story Conor was telling when I noticed Dylan staring intently at my chest. I cleared my throat. His attention lingered then rose to my face.

I mouthed a quick, *What?*

Are you wearing a bra? he mouthed back.

Instantly, my nipples hardened at the thought of him studying me, trying to decide if I was wearing one. My T-shirt was extra baggy, and I wore a small vest underneath, so it wasn't immediately obvious. I simply cocked a brow at him and ignored his mouthed question. He knocked back a long gulp of beer and frowned. Maybe he was annoyed that I wasn't wearing a bra and he couldn't do anything about it.

"Jeez, it's getting late. I better call a taxi," Conor announced. "You ready to head back, Dylan?"

Dylan cast me frustrated look, then brought his attention to Conor. "Sure, why not."

A few minutes later their taxi arrived. Dylan came and gave me a quick kiss on the cheek before they left, whispering in my ear, "You just love to torture me."

I only smiled in return and then they were gone.

"I'm going to bed," Yvonne said, yawning.

"Go ahead. I'll clean up out here."

My phone buzzed with a text when I was in the kitchen. I picked it up.

Dylan: Wish I could've stayed over again. I missed you last night.

I thought about how to reply. He was being too romantic, and I couldn't handle it. I already felt like I was falling for him way too quickly, which was why I responded with humour.

Evelyn: Boob oglers don't get to stay over.

Dylan: Not even if they pay fealty to said boobs?

Evelyn: I'd advise you to remove 'pay fealty' from your dirty talk repertoire.

Dylan: Too medieval?

Evelyn: Makes me think of a nerdy guy in a cosplay outfit who wants to be dominated.

Dylan: Enough said. It's out.

Dylan: Just out of curiosity, what should be in my repertoire?

Evelyn: I can't give you answers to the test. That's cheating :-P

Dylan: Just looking for some pointers.

Evelyn: Okay, here's one: Go to bed. You have work in the morning.

Dylan: Have you thought any more about Saturday?

I hesitated before typing out a reply.

Evelyn: I'll go, but only because I want to see the farm.

Dylan: Great. I'll pick you up at 10. Xxx

A few minutes went by and I was just climbing into bed when my phone buzzed again.

Dylan: I know I already said it, but you really did look beautiful tonight.

I swallowed down the flutters his text solicited and typed back.

Evelyn: And you looked very handsome.

Dylan: See you Saturday, Ev.

Evelyn: See you Saturday, Dylan.

I slid my phone onto my dresser, switched off the lamp and closed my eyes, a smile on my face as I fell asleep.

Twelve

"Is this your car?" I asked Dylan when he picked me up outside my building on Saturday morning.

I slid into the passenger seat, enjoying the feel of the soft leather. I knew nothing about cars, but I could tell this one was expensive, and I bet it wasn't even on a payment plan. Seemed you could buy expensive cars when you were the master of your own universe. Sometimes it freaked me out how far Dylan had come in life. Okay, a lot of the time it freaked me out, but I was slowly getting used to it.

"Yeah, bit of a pain in the arse though," he replied. "There are all these rules about parking here. I have to send my assistant over to move it at different times of the day."

"You have an assistant?"

He nodded. "His name's Clive. Good bloke."

That was interesting. I never saw him around, but then again, I'd only visited Dylan at work twice. "Clive is such an assistant's name."

Dylan shot me a funny look as he pulled into traffic. "Is it?"

"Yep. I can just imagine you all, *Clive, get me my coffee. Clive, tell Nancy in accounting I can't make our 11:05. Clive, bring me my navy pea coat.*"

Dylan's husky laugh sent a pleasurable shiver down my spine. "First of all, I don't shout commands at him, I ask nicely. And second of all, I have never worn a pea coat in my life."

"Don't believe you for a second. I bet you have several in various shades of businessman," I taunted.

His lips twitched as he narrowed his gaze, looking between the road and me. There was heavy traffic, so it was going to take us a while to get out of Brooklyn.

"You're hilarious."

I smiled wide. "Why thanks."

Reaching out, I turned on the radio and Taylor Swift's new song came on. Dylan chuckled when I shimmied my shoulders and sang along.

"I take it you're a fan?"

I shrugged. "It's catchy."

"You're a delight."

I grinned and continued my sing-a-long.

"How's your dad these days?" I asked when we finally got out of the city. Dylan hadn't mentioned his dad yet, and I wondered if everything was okay with him.

"Really good, actually. He's still in Galway. I bought him a house down there."

"You did? That's great."

"He likes having his own space. He's even started seeing a woman named Bridget. He calls her his friend, but I know better."

"That sly dog," I said with a laugh.

"I'm just happy he's happy." Dylan glanced at me for a second. "What about your mam? Do you see her much?"

I pursed my lips and let out a sigh. "Nope. I'm pretty sure that's a dead relationship. I know they say you only get one set of parents, or one single parent in my case, but sometimes you just have to accept that they aren't worth the heartache." I paused to look out the window, not saying anything for a minute. "I guess I got a little colder after Sam died. I decided I wasn't going to waste my time and energy on people who didn't deserve it anymore. It was probably the only good thing that came of his death."

Dylan frowned and went quiet in that way he always did whenever I mentioned Sam.

He cleared his throat, his voice solemn when he said, "Do you ever wonder where he'd be now if he was still with us?"

I swallowed and fiddled with the sleeve of my jacket. "I like to hope he would've come here with me."

"He'd have loved New York." Dylan smiled fondly.

"I know," I said, my own smile sad. "I just have to think he's in a better place now, looking down on us all and judging our life choices. Well, maybe not yours, because you obviously make great ones, but he'd definitely have a lot to say about mine."

Dylan shook his head and stared at the road. I felt like he wanted to say something, but was holding back. I reached out to touch his arm.

"What is it?"

He exhaled and glanced at me, eyes skimming my forehead and nose, my lips. "It frustrates me how down you are on yourself."

"It's just the truth. I mean, I've never done anything meaningful. Not like you."

Dylan flexed his hand where it rested on the steering wheel. When he spoke, his voice was tense. "How is anything I've done more meaningful than you caring for your grandmother? Putting your own happiness aside for the sake of her health?"

"I never saw it as putting my own happiness aside. It was just something I was meant to do," I said quietly.

Dylan glanced at me, then reached for my hand and gave it a brief squeeze. "Every year around this time, I've thought about flying to Ireland and finally convincing you to come back with me, but I never did. You know why?"

I shook my head.

"Because I knew despite my own selfish need to be with you, you were living a worthwhile life. You were doing something that made a world of difference for one person, and that was enough." *Wow. That's how he saw me?*

His words made me emotional. "I guess."

"So please, don't compare us like I'm this big success and you're a failure, because it's simply not true. Who you are as a human is its own success."

My throat was tight as I stared at my lap. It was ridiculous, but I wanted to cry. It just felt so nice to have someone tell me that. To let me know I was doing okay. That I didn't need to achieve particular things, I just needed to do what felt right for me.

It was almost lunch when we arrived at the farm. Dylan pulled up to a large brick house where Frank stood on the porch. Unlike the suit he wore the other night at the gala, now he wore jeans, a green shirt, and a ball cap covered his grey hair.

He brought us inside and fed us tomato soup with grilled cheese sandwiches before giving us our tour. My heart filled with longing when I saw his workers in the fields.

That could be me, I thought to myself.

It was the first time I realised that my head told me not to garden, but deep at the back of my heart, there was a place that still yearned to sink my fingers into soil, plant seeds that would transform into something pretty and bright.

That place grew bigger each day, and it was all because of Dylan.

"Do you mind if we take a little walk around before we head back?" Dylan asked when we came to the end of our tour.

"Not at all," Frank replied, then looked to me. "And Evelyn, if you ever need a job you know where to find me."

"Thank you. That's very kind."

Frank shook his head. "I'd be lucky to have you. I could see your passion for growing while we walked through the flower beds. It's not something people can fake."

He left us and a warmth seized my chest at his words. Was it so clear to see my old love for gardening?

Dylan took my hand and we walked in quiet for a little while, until we reached a small storehouse, where pretty winter jasmine vines crawled up a trellis.

"I love this colour yellow," I said, admiring the flowers as I bent to take a sniff.

"I use these in *E.V.* you know," Dylan said, reaching out to touch the petals.

"Oh, and what else?" I asked, unable to help my curiosity.

His expression grew amused. "I keep forgetting you've never smelled it."

"Is that funny?"

He didn't answer, and instead listed the ingredients. "*E.V.* is mostly made up of jasmine, echinacea and wildflower top notes, angelica root for the middle note and anise hyssop for the base."

I frowned at him, because that sounded a lot like the perfume he made when we were still at school, the one he'd used my flowers to create. Dylan must've seen the realisation on my face.

"Ah, now she gets it."

"*E.V.* is that same perfume you made in the lab at our school?"

"With a few adjustments here and there."

"Wow, that's . . . wow."

I didn't know what to say. I couldn't believe that something so simple, a little school chemistry project making perfume, could turn into a global success. Dylan tugged on my hand and we continued walking. "It's still my best work. I think that's because I made it when I was with you."

My mind wandered back to what he'd called me when we slept together, and heat suffused my chest.

My muse.

"So, I'm your lucky charm?"

He grinned. "Something like that."

We walked for a few more minutes then headed back to the house. When we reached the car, Dylan hesitated at the driver's side. I stood on the passenger's side and studied him. He looked like he was deep in thought.

"Everything okay?"

He fiddled with his keys and pressed the button to unlock the doors, but he didn't move to open it. I didn't open mine either, wondering what he was thinking about. I didn't have to wonder long when he braced his hands on the roof of the car and levelled his eyes on me.

"I want us to design a perfume together."

His statement took me completely off guard as I stared at him, wide-eyed. "You and me?"

"Yes. And I want to dedicate it to Sam."

I swallowed a few times as emotion clutched me. The idea of doing something like that after all these years . . .

I blinked to keep from welling up. "But I don't know anything about designing perfume."

"Yes, you do. You've just pushed it to the back of your mind. All you need to do is rediscover it."

I knew he was talking about my allotment, the flowers I used to grow. I guess I did know a little about perfume in the sense that I knew what almost every flower smelled like. Even now, I could pick them out the moment I stepped into a room, whether it was a rose-scented candle or the orange blossom in a bowl of potpourri on a coffee table.

"Why do you want to do this?" I asked.

Dylan appeared overcome. "I just . . . I know this sounds ridiculous, because I was at his funeral, but I feel like I never really got to say goodbye. He was there one minute and gone the next. Sam was such a vibrant soul, and I feel like the world needs to know he existed, even if he was taken too soon."

And you blame yourself, I thought.

I knew he'd never admit it, but it was true. Those boys had been after Dylan, not Sam. He was caught in the crossfire, and paid the ultimate price. I thought of how angry I'd been back then, how angry Dylan was, too.

I stifled the need to cry for a second time and walked around the car. Without a word, I pulled him into a hug and he practically melted into my arms. I could feel his vulnerability like a tangible thing. I rubbed his back and nuzzled my nose into his neck.

I felt him shiver and wrap his arms around my waist. He held me tight as I whispered in his ear one word. "Okay."

***

"So anyway, we have two kids and neither of us wants more. My wife asked me to have a vasectomy, because the labour with our second was so awful and she never wants to go through that again," said the man sitting in front of me.

I was working my usual shift at the bar, and listening to the woes of customers came with the job.

Most of the time, I didn't mind, but tonight my head was elsewhere. I was too busy thinking about Dylan's proposal. Design a perfume together.

I knew it wasn't some ploy to spend more time with me, because I'd always been able to tell when he was being honest. Not that he'd ever been dishonest. Anyway, I'd agreed to do it, but now I wondered what I'd gotten myself into.

On the drive home he told me that he'd pay me for my time, and that we'd donate half of the profits to charities that worked to keep young kids out of gangs. I was touched that he was willing to do that, but also by the sentiment. He'd obviously spent a lot of time thinking it all through.

"I really want to do it for her, but I keep hearing stories about men who feel different afterward. Like they're obsolete, not a man anymore."

I brought my attention back to my customer. "How old are you?"

"Twenty-seven."

I pursed my lips. "That's very young. I'm not sure any doctors will agree to the procedure."

"Maggie's determined. She could nag any doctor into submission. I feel like I'm being bullied into it."

I nodded sympathetically just as Yvonne walked out of the back office.

"I think you should tell your wife what you just told me. If she loves you, she'll understand," I said then walked to the other end of the bar to meet my aunt.

"Working late?" I asked as she slid onto a stool and let out a tired sigh.

"Yes. We need to start hiring some extra staff for the run up to Christmas. I spent half the day putting up advertisements online."

I bit my lip, feeling bad about what I was going to say next. "Speaking of staff, I may need to cut down on my hours for a little while."

"Why? Did you get another job?"

"Sort of. Dylan's asked me to help him with his next perfume."

Yvonne's eyes widened. "Really? That's amazing."

"He wants to dedicate it to Sam and donate half the profits to charity," I continued.

"Oh my."

"Oh my is right. Every time I try to keep my emotions out of things with Dylan, he goes and does something that just melts my flipping heart. It's too much."

"He's a very special person, Ev. You're lucky to have him."

I flinched, because her words were so similar to what Laura said at the gala the other night, though the meaning behind them was completely different. Then I remembered what Dylan said to me in the car earlier, and how convinced Frank had been that my passion was easy to read. *Others see me so differently than how I see myself.* Moments like these, I wondered if a lot of my feelings of unworthiness stemmed from Mam leaving me.

But I shook my head. No, not anymore. I've had people validate me my whole life. Yvonne, Sam, now Dylan . . . or rather, Dylan *again.*

I had to live my life for me—*be me*—nothing more, nothing less. *Who you are as a human is its own success.* I wasn't obligated to impress or appease anyone with achievements.

I sniffled and glanced back at Yvonne. "So, you don't mind if I cut my hours?"

"Not at all. I'll just hire some extra Christmas workers in the meantime."

"Have I ever told you you're the best?"

She smiled. "Not recently, but feel free. Also, I'll have a glass of merlot. It's been a long day."

I smiled back at her. "Coming right up."

Thirteen

Dylan: SOS. I need your help.

Evelyn: Oh no! Did you get your Johnson stuck in your fly?

Dylan: What? No. How is that the first thing you thought of?

Evelyn: I heard it's a common predicament for gentlemen.

Several weeks went by and Dylan and I started tentatively working on our scent. We were still in the ideas phase, so we hadn't really settled on anything yet. Most of the time we just hung out, either at my place or his, sometimes in his office, and talked about anything and everything. In between the anything and everything was where the ideas sprung to life.

It excited me to talk about flowers again, to think about the scents we could use and the possible combinations. I wondered what Sam would think of it all. He'd probably tell us to stop being all mushy and sentimental, but secretly love the attention.

Dylan was becoming as familiar to me as he'd been when we were teenagers, except without the sex. After that one night, he'd allowed me to set the pace. He never pushed for anything other than what I was prepared to give, which just kind of melted my heart. Though admittedly, it was agonising to be around him and not, you know . . . *do* things. *Especially when he kissed me goodbye. How we'd pulled away breathless time after time. It had almost killed me to send him away. Every. Time.*

The problem was, sex made everything complicated. It made me feel like my emotions were running the show, rather than my head, and I wasn't ready to give up that sort of control.

Dylan: Well, thankfully I've never had that problem. I need you to clear your schedule this Saturday to come Christmas shopping with me.

Evelyn: Why can't you be a normal person and shop online?

Dylan: Because I prefer to shop in person. Also, my dad's coming to visit and he's bringing Bridget. I need your help finding her a gift.

God, could he be any more adorable?

Evelyn: How exciting. Okay, I'm in.

Dylan: You have an odd definition of excitement.

Evelyn: No, I don't. I'm putting my money on her being a hot twenty-something with a thing for older men.

Dylan: I hate you.

Evelyn: Mwah ha ha. Okay sorry. That was evil.

Dylan: You're forgiven. See you Saturday.

I paired my cosiest black yoga pants with a long burgundy woollen jumper before heading out to meet Dylan for our planned shopping trip. I figured I'd kill two birds with one stone and do something Christmas shopping of my own. Not that I had a whole bunch of people to buy for, just Yvonne and Dylan. Maybe Conor, too.

I also wanted to buy decorations for the apartment. There was another week before people put up their trees, but I wanted to be prepared. Maybe I'd get one of those mini trees with the fake snow and lights.

Dylan stood by the entrance to the department store wearing a long black coat, a navy scarf and leather gloves. He was probably wearing the most clothes I'd ever seen him in, and yet, he managed to look sexier than I'd ever seen him look. It was ridiculous. And unfair.

I wanted to grab him by that sexy scarf and pull him into a private corner.

"Could this city be any more Christmassy? Usually, I'm such a Grinch, but all these twinkle lights are really putting me in the mood," I said as I approached.

He grinned and arched an eyebrow. "In the mood, huh?"

I slapped him on the shoulder. "Get your mind out of the gutter."

His answering chuckle was smooth as chocolate. "Hey, you make it too easy."

I slid my arm through his as we walked inside. "So, here's the deal, we can get your gifts here, but afterward you have to come downtown with me."

"There's lots of affordable stuff here," Dylan argued.

"We'll see," I grumbled.

"If you can't find anything, I promise to take you *downtown*."

He winked, a twinkle in his eye and I narrowed my gaze. I elbowed him in the side, about to reply when I was distracted.

"Oh my God, is that a chocolate fountain?"

I led him to a window display and Dylan chuckled. "Let's do our shopping first and then we can get excited about chocolate fountains."

My only response was an overly dramatic frown and sad puppy eyes.

He pulled me along. "You're cute. We can come back this way when we're done."

Over an hour later we'd managed to find something for everyone. Dylan bought a cashmere scarf for Bridget, a new watch for his dad, and some brightly coloured socks for Conor. I got Yvonne a Gucci perfume set that was on sale, mostly to rile Dylan, plus some glitzy decorations for the apartment. I didn't need to go anywhere else after all.

We were still in the cosmetics section when Dylan paused in front of the perfume counter. There was a collection of testers on display, one of which was *E.V.* Dylan shot me a sneaky glance.

"I'll take this one," he said to the girl. She didn't bat an eyelid, only nodded and rang up the purchase.

Like most perfume designers, the majority of people knew the brand name *Dylan*, but they didn't know what he looked like, not unless they were in the biz. I mean, I had no idea what Issey Miyake looked like, or Paco Rabanne, but I knew their names. I guess that was a good thing. It meant Dylan could still live a moderately normal life. I definitely didn't think he'd enjoy all the pomp and ceremony of being famous.

He came back to me and held out the bag. I quirked a brow.

"Why on earth did you just buy a bottle of your own perfume?"

His smile was infectious. "It's an early Christmas gift. Here, take it."

I stared at the bag. "You could've just given me a bottle from your shop."

"Well, this way it's a proper gift that I paid for," he said, coming to place the bag over my arm with the others.

I blinked. For some strange reason, I was extremely touched by the gesture. Looking away, I walked over to another counter, feigning interest in some face cream.

"You'll have to tell me what you think when you try it," Dylan said, standing next to me. I was struck with an urge to reach out and take his hand in mine, twine our fingers together.

"Sure, I'll let you know."

"Your opinion is very important to me, Evelyn."

"And yours is important to me," I whispered, still not looking at him.

We stood like that for a minute, side by side, just letting the noise of shoppers wash over us. When I finally glanced up, Dylan's eyes almost brimmed over with affection. My heart skipped a beat. I couldn't believe we were sharing this oddly intense moment in the middle of a busy department store. It was moments like this, when even though we were surrounded by many I felt as though I was alone with Dylan, that I saw how easily we fit together. *He'd become my best friend again.* Friend. Dylan was way more than that, but for now . . .

I cleared my throat and stepped away. "We should go get pizza."

"Pizza?"

"Yes, believe it or not, I haven't eaten any New York pizza yet. I'm pretty sure it's some kind of sacrilegious offence."

Dylan chuckled softly. "In that case, follow me. I know just the place."

***

"Oh my God."

"I know."

"No, seriously."

"Seriously."

"This is so good."

"It's the best."

"I never knew you could make heaven with only three ingredients."

We stood outside a tiny hole-in-the-wall pizza place, devouring our little slices of heaven. I finished mine off in record time and wiped my mouth with a napkin.

"I'm still hungry. We should get hotdogs for dessert."

Instead of arguing that they weren't dessert food, Dylan simply nodded his agreement and hailed a taxi. We were dropped off outside Central Park, purchased two hotdogs, then wandered inside for a stroll. We just finished eating when we came upon a small flower stall. I was attracted to the poinsettias, moving to admire them. Dylan joined me and bent to breathe them in. His expression turned thoughtful as he urged me to smell them, too.

They smelled very, very faintly of pine and something quite vague underneath, something that reminded me weirdly of turpentine. I said as much to Dylan.

"Well, turpentine comes from pine trees, and poinsettias have a pine-like scent so . . ."

I studied him as his words trailed off, thoughts racing behind his eyes.

"What are you thinking?"

Those eyes came back to me. "Remember during our brainstorm last week, when we thought about combining freesias with fig leaf and tiare flowers? I think this is the missing link."

Freesias had always been Sam's favourite, which was why I'd suggested them. Everything else we'd chosen was to complement their sweet, honey-like scent.

"We'd need to smell them all together to be sure," I said, invigorated by his sudden enthusiasm. There was liveliness in his expression I hadn't yet seen, a creative flow.

Without a word he went and purchased a bunch of poinsettias from the lady manning the stall, and before I knew it we were in a taxi heading to his house. We still had all our shopping with us, and it was probably about time I got home, but I was too curious to see if Dylan was right about the poinsettias. I'd become thoroughly invested in creating this perfume and I wanted it to be incredible just as he did.

When we arrived at his place, Conor was out. I set my bags on the floor and flopped onto the couch, exhausted after being on my feet all day. Dylan went into the kitchen. I could hear him moving around and it sounded like he was digging in the cupboards. When my curiosity got the best of me, I finally dragged myself off the couch and went to investigate.

Dylan had some sort of copper contraption all set up on the counter. It reminded me a little of those Turkish water pipes they have in cafes.

"What is that?" I asked and stepped closer to take a look.

"It's a copper alembic. I use it to distil my own essential oils."

"Oh," I said, intrigued. I took a stool and watched as he fiddled around with it, adding water and setting it to boil. "Do you make all your own essential oils for your perfumes?"

"For the initial designing process, yes. Usually, I have a lab to do all this. I've been meaning to rent one while I'm here, but I haven't had the chance."

He glanced at me for a second, his gaze heated and my chest warmed.

I brought my attention to the copper contraption. "So, how does it work?"

Dylan gestured to the part that boiled the water. "Steam distillation extracts the aromatic compounds from the plant. The combination of heated steam and pressure helps release the essential oil from its microscopic protective sacs. The vapor mixture flows through the condenser and cools, creating a layer of oil and a layer of water. The oil rises to the top and is separated from the flower water and collected, which is the part we're after."

I nodded, weirdly aroused by all this science talk. What was wrong with me?

"How long does it take?"

"Depends on the plant, but usually about a day, give or take."

"That's a long time."

His lips twitched at my groan. "Which is why I was so keen to start the process."

"Well, what the hell are we gonna do while we wait?"

He smirked. "I can think of a few things."

I narrowed my gaze and tried not to smile. "I bet you can."

We stayed locked in a moment until the door opened and Conor walked in. My skin beaded everywhere Dylan looked, even though I was wearing a giant knitted jumper.

"Hey Ev. I didn't know you were coming over," Conor greeted cheerily as he came inside.

I blinked and turned away from Dylan. "It was spur of the moment thing, but I actually have to get going," I said and went to collect my shopping bags.

"Tell Yvonne I said hi."

"Will do."

Dylan, ever the gentleman, grabbed my coat as I picked up the shopping and was ready to put it on me when I got to the door. He leaned down to kiss my cheek.

"I wish you could stay. I don't feel as though I've had enough time with you today."

"We've been together all day, Dylan," I chided with a smile, but I knew what he meant. It was so easy to be with him, and I didn't want to leave either if I was being honest. Still, it was better to go than stay and just want more and more time with him. He only continued to stare at me, all tender and warm. I cleared my throat.

"I need to get home, but thank you for an incredible day. My first Christmas shopping in New York. It was as magical as I hoped."

"The pleasure was mine." He kissed my lips softly, and I didn't want to step back. I wanted to step forwards into his arms and be held and caressed. I wanted to be engulfed by him. I loved his respect for me, but a part of me hated it too. *This is the right thing for now, Ev. The right thing for you.*

"I'll see you soon?"

"Yes, love. Let me know when you're home," he added in his best father voice. *He always knew when to bring a moment of humour.*

"Yes, Dad," I said, chuckling.

When I did get home, I went straight to my bedroom, exhausted. I changed into PJs, sent Dylan a quick text, then made myself some tea. I wasn't really hungry after the whole pizza followed by hotdogs indulgence. Crawling into bed, I replayed the day's events in my head, unable to stop thinking about Dylan when he discovered the poinsettias. He'd been enthused, full of life, his entire form vibrating with creative energy.

Then I remembered him buying me the perfume as an early Christmas gift. Curiosity got the better of me and I climbed out of bed, opened my wardrobe and pulled out the small gift bag. I tore away the protective plastic and opened the box to remove the bottle of *E.V.* My hand shook as I uncapped it and pressed down on the nozzle.

Scent filled the room and I closed my eyes, inhaling deeply. My pores tingled, the hairs on my arms stood on end, and every part of my heart filled with memories. This was the perfume Dylan made at school, only better. The scent was . . . sophisticated where once there'd been the naivety of a novice.

It was . . . glorious, sumptuous, a medley of wonder.

Pictures flashed in my head, all solicited from the bold notes of jasmine, the sweetness of the echinacea and the sudden pop of anise.

I saw us on the roof of the Villas, so young and innocent, falling in love.

I saw us spending every day together, full of passion and excitement to have found someone that fit us so perfectly.

It amazed me how something so simple, just a combination of scents could propel me through a porthole into the past. And if I concentrated hard enough, I could pretend I was back there, just for a little while.

I could be in a place where I was happy, a moment captured in time, before everything changed.

Fourteen

"I got your text," I said as I entered Dylan's office.

He stood by his desk, a mess of tubes containing different essential oils in front of him. There were notes scribbled on paper and discarded paper coffee cups galore. He looked manic and exhausted. His shirtsleeves were rolled up, the top few buttons of his shirt undone. His hair was rumpled in a way that made me want to run my hands through it and mess it up even more.

"Great, you're here. Come in," he said and ushered me forward.

I unbuttoned my coat and slipped it off, wondering what he was in such a hurry for.

"What's going on, Dylan?"

He levelled his eyes on me, his brimming over with frenetic energy. "I think I've found it."

"Found what?"

"The combination of scents."

"Oh," I exclaimed. "That's fantastic. Can I smell?

"Of course. Why do you think I asked you over?" Dylan picked up a container and started adding lots of different oils. He placed them in an odd little machine that mixed them all up, then he removed the container and held it out to me.

I eyed him curiously. "You don't want to smell it first?"

He shook his head. "No. It has to be you. I want to see your reaction, then I'll know if it's right."

This felt like an important moment.

He was bestowing a responsibility on me—*an honour*—that I wasn't sure I was worthy of. Swallowing back my nerves, I took it from him.

I inhaled and closed my eyes. A medley of freesia, fig leaf, tiare flower and poinsettia captured my senses. It was the original mixture we'd come up with together, but there was more and it was all Dylan. I would never have the nose, the creative intuition and genius to pick out such a perfect combination. Sam's smile flashed in my mind's eye, his blue eyes shining in a moment of happiness, and I knew Dylan had gotten it right. There was orchid and vanilla and something else . . .

"Is that pepper?"

"Yes," Dylan exclaimed, his smile huge, eyes so alight they practically sparkled.

I concentrated, trying hard to figure out the base note. "And sandalwood?"

"Perfect," he breathed.

"You took the words right out of my mouth."

"No, I mean your reaction. It's perfect. That's exactly what I wanted to see."

"You can tell if a perfume's right from just one person's reaction?"

"Not just anybody's. Yours."

My cheeks reddened as I set the container down on his desk. "So, what next?"

Dylan started to pace, his mind moving faster than his words. "I'll have my lab in California create a number of samples. We'll test them on my marketing

186

team, collect their responses and ideas. After that we'll figure out what direction we want to take."

I stared at him, feeling truly hopeful and inspired for the first time in a long time.

"I'm excited," I breathed.

He came and stood in front of me, then pulled me close to his chest with his arms wrapped around me. "We did it, Ev." He almost sounded like a giddy little boy, but hints of sadness permeated his excitement as if he still wasn't sure it was enough. *It is enough, Dylan. It is. You are.*

He pulled back and took each of my hands in his. "Thank you."

He kissed my forehead, lingering a little longer than perhaps necessary when he said, "I've been meaning to ask, what are your and Yvonne's plans for Christmas?"

I gave a gentle shrug. "We'll probably just hang out at the apartment and gorge on turkey. Why?"

His expression softened. "What do you think about coming to stay at my place? My dad and Bridget will be there, and Conor's parents and his sister, Bethany, are coming, too."

My heart swelled, because that sounded lovely. I'd never had a big family Christmas in a houseful of people before. For so long it had been Yvonne and me, then Gran and me if Yvonne couldn't make it home to visit.

I looked up at Dylan and nodded. "Sure, I'll ask Yvonne, but I'm sure she'd love to."

His answering smile took my breath away.

***

It was Christmas Eve morning when Dylan and I were scheduled to meet with his marketing team. I thought it was an odd day to do it, but Dylan said he wanted to get the ball rolling so we could go full steam ahead in the new year.

I turned up at the offices, which happened to be located in Manhattan. They were on the 47th floor of a building on Park Avenue and I swore my ears popped going up in the elevator. I wore the only black pencil skirt I owned, with a deep red blouse and some heels. I hoped I looked the part and didn't immediately give off 'outsider' vibes.

Dylan met me at reception and led me into a long meeting room where a bunch of well-dressed people waited. They chatted amongst themselves and sipped on coffees when we stepped inside.

"I'm nervous," I whispered to him.

"Don't be. You'll do fine," Dylan reassured and gave my hand a quick squeeze.

"Mr O'Dea, we're very excited to sample the newest scent," said a dark-haired woman wearing a navy fitted dress. She looked to be in her early thirties and was extremely attractive.

"Ah, Miss Keating, can I introduce you to Evelyn Flynn? She collaborated with me on the scent. Ev, this is Diana Keating, Head of Marketing."

Her eyes met mine with interest and curiosity, probably because Dylan had never collaborated with anyone before.

"It's a pleasure to meet you, Evelyn," she said and offered her hand. We shook as she went on, "And which perfumes have you worked on in the past?"

"Oh, this is my first," I replied, stomach twisting. Here came the judgement. I could feel it rolling in on a tidal wave of self-importance.

"How wonderful, good for you." She might as well have said, *You're not good enough for this company. I don't know what Dylan was thinking bringing you on board.* Some women had a skill for saying so much more than the words that came out of their mouths. It was all in the tone.

"Evelyn is a very talented gardener. She grew the flowers I used in my very first perfume," Dylan said. I noticed this was something he liked to tell people to give me a little boost of confidence, and it worked. Already Diana's judgement simmered down, though I suspected she had a bit of a thing for Dylan. It was in the way she played with her hair and swayed her hips when she walked toward him.

Damn, were we all that obvious when attracted to someone? I hoped I wasn't because that shit was embarrassing.

"Well, I'm very much looking forward to what you both came up with," said Diana and we all sat. I was introduced to the other members of Dylan's marketing team, before he stood and opened a leather briefcase. Inside were seven bottles, all containing the same list of ingredients, but with different combinations of each.

These people were our test subjects, so we could find which variation was the most appealing. After each bottle was a small dish of coffee beans to help identify each option better. Smelling coffee beans between perfume samples increased the ability to perceive different aromas as opposed to smelling air between each sample.

It was all very interesting, so much so that I forgot about Diana's interest in Dylan while the samples were being passed around. Everyone was given the chance to smell each one, then air their opinion. Dylan's assistant, Clive, sat in the far corner of the room recording what was said for later use.

When all bottles had been sampled, Dylan opened up the room to further discussion. We were both keen to know which one was everybody's favourite.

"Number three has a spike of musk at the end that I think our customers will find too strong," said one woman. "But number six has just the right amount of floral to green to spiciness. It's definitely my favourite."

"I agree about number six," someone else added. "There's a herbal note within the floral that's very unique."

"Yes, and I don't think I've ever encountered a perfume with a poinsettia note before. It's very unusual, subtle yet so unexpected, but somehow it just works."

I smiled, because again Dylan found that one thing to make the perfume—*our* perfume—special, and it was completely by accident. If I hadn't suggested going for hotdogs, we might never have walked by that flower stall, and then we wouldn't have discovered the missing link.

"I'm interested to see how the scent fades in a couple of hours," Diana said. "That will be the telling part."

"Oh, I wore it home the other day and it only gets better," I replied. "The spiciness of the sandalwood comes out with the sweetness of the vanilla. It's very pleasant."

She took in what I said, but instead of responding to me, she turned her attention to Dylan. "Sounds like another success story, Mr O'Dea. As soon as we return after the holidays I'll get straight to work developing a marketing strategy."

"Perfect, thank you."

Someone cleared their throat, a man sitting at the very end of the long table. I remembered he'd also favoured number six. "I hope you don't mind me asking, but has it been given a name yet?"

Dylan smiled then looked to me when he answered poignantly. "Yes, we've decided to name it *Samuel*."

Fifteen

"That Diana fancies the pants off you," I commented when we left the offices. Dylan had offered to drive me back to my apartment. I still needed to pack for staying over at his house the next two nights, though he was sure to mention Yvonne and I would be sleeping in one of the guest bedrooms.

"You're imagining things."

"I am not. She wants you."

He sighed heavily. "She's very good at her job."

"Hey, I'm not telling you to fire her, just stating a fact. I think you can be a little oblivious to these things," I teased to lighten the mood.

"I can tell when a woman is attracted to me, Evelyn."

"Well, Diana's admiration definitely escaped your attention."

His voice was a low, soothing rumble that hit me right in the pit of the stomach. "Maybe I was just too busy looking at you."

I rubbed my palms along my skirt and wet my suddenly dry lips. What he said rendered me a little hot and bothered.

His expression was thoughtful when he went on. "Believe it or not, Laura was the only employee I ever slept with. I don't make a habit of it."

I touched his hand, appreciating him wanting me to know it wasn't something he did often, or ever.

"I believe you."

He glanced between the road and me. "I just want to make sure you're aware . . ." He trailed off.

"Aware?"

He huffed a frustrated breath. "I want to make sure you're aware that you're the only person I want to be with. I don't notice how other women look at me, Ev. I only notice you."

I held still. His declaration was so unexpected and out of the blue. It wasn't that I was unaware he wanted me, it was just that in the last few weeks, we'd worked on being friendly and not really saying what we felt. About each other, anyway.

My voice was so, so quiet when I responded. "I feel the same way."

Silence filled the car. I looked at the passing buildings, the Christmas lights and people rushing around buying last-minute gifts. Something about the moment, being here with Dylan, just felt . . . right.

Without warning, he reached out and lifted my hand, bringing my wrist to his nose so he could inhale. I'd sprayed a little of number six on during the sampling session.

"Your skin was made to smell beautiful," he murmured.

"*Samuel* is a very beautiful scent."

His eyes met mine, the car stopped in traffic. "You approve of the name?"

Almost instantly, tears sprung in my eyes. "Of course. It's perfect."

I sniffled and looked away again. The traffic let up and we made our way across the Brooklyn Bridge. I

193

thought of the gift Dylan bought me during our shopping trip the other week. He'd never asked me what I thought, even though I sensed it meant a lot to him to know.

I didn't think when I blurted, "I think *E.V.* smells best when it fades."

Dylan seemed to hold his breath. Was he surprised? He exhaled and there was a long few moments before he spoke. He nodded as he kept his eyes on the road. "It meshes with the wearer, becomes a part of them."

I mustered the courage to continue. "Some perfumes don't do that though. It takes skill, I think. Some fade and become unpleasant, but yours get better the longer you wear them. We might've come up with the idea for *Samuel* together, but you're the one who made it special. You're the reason why all those people in that room today were so impressed."

Dylan shook his head, his eyes ablaze. "I might create them, but they're all you."

My heart stuttered in my chest. "What do you mean?"

"Each perfume I've create was inspired by you, Ev. *Synaesthesia* is you in the morning, when you've just woken up. *Wildflower* is you when you dance. *E.V* is you when you smile. *Limerence* is how I love you. And *Hiraeth* is how I've felt for eleven years without you in my life."

I was short of breath, mouth agape. He always used such fancy, romantic words to name his scents. One night I'd looked up their meanings.

Synaesthesia was feeling a sense outside of the one stimulated, like seeing colour in sound, or hearing sound in colour.

Limerence was euphoric love.

And *Hiraeth* was a Welsh word for homesickness, for a place you could never return to.

Suddenly, it all made sense. But Dylan was wrong. Each perfume wasn't me. Each perfume was *us*. Together, they told our story.

I swallowed, my body aquiver as I asked, "What does *E.V.* stand for?"

He reached out and took my hand in his, twining our fingers together as his eyes captured mine. "It doesn't stand for anything. How could I create a perfume for a girl I love and not give it her name?"

Liquid pooled in my eyes, while emotion caught in my throat. I saw the stark, blatant honesty in his words and mourned for all the time we'd lost. Mourned because I had been lost *in* mourning. We both had been. *He* had to leave when he did. *I* had to stay when he left. Our paths diverged, first one, then two.

Now they'd collided once more. I wanted to say something, but I knew Dylan would be all right with my silence. I needed to process his words, and he knew me well enough to allow that. I wanted to tell him I'd never stopped loving him and had lost hope of ever knowing love again. But I remained quiet. In awe. Feeling overwhelmed with gratitude for whoever put our meeting in New York into place.

Dylan pulled his car to a stop outside my building. He slid his fingers through mine and for a few minutes we simply sat there.

"When will you be over later?" he asked, voice soft.

"Yvonne finishes work at five, so we'll head over together then."

He lifted our twined fingers to his mouth and pressed a kiss to the top of my hand. "I'll see you then."

Inside the apartment, I felt like I was floating on air the entire time I packed. I could've put nothing but socks inside my overnight bag and I'd be none the wiser. Dylan's tender words kept replaying in my head. I should've kissed him right there in his car. I should've dragged him inside and thrown him down on my bed.

The way he felt for me, how honest and truthful and kind he was, he deserved to be cherished. He deserved someone who could love him just as much as he loved them. I wanted to be that person so badly, but I questioned my ability to love as openly as he did. To give all of myself, because life and loss had hardened me.

I was still completely immersed in this thought spiral when the door opened and shut. Yvonne was home, a cheerful smile on her face.

"Happy Christmas Eve!" she sing-songed and came over to give me a hug. Her joy was infectious, and I smiled despite myself.

"You're in a good mood."

"I'm off work for the next three days and we're going to stay in a big fancy townhouse. How could I not be full of seasonal cheer?"

I chuckled. "Do you need time to pack?"

"Nope. Already took care of it last night. So, tell me, how did the meeting go this morning?"

My smile grew bigger. "It went great. They loved the scent."

"I can't wait to see how it all turns out. I bet Dylan's planning something extra special."

"You mean for when it releases?"

"Yes, that ad he put in the newspaper for his last perfume was stunning."

I chewed on my lip. "I hadn't even thought of that. I'm just so glad we managed to come up with something together. I'm really starting to feel . . ." I trailed off, my heart squeezing.

"Happy?" Yvonne finished.

I blinked a few times, overcome with emotion, then nodded. "Yes, happy."

It was such a simple concept, but it was something I'd been striving for, yet hadn't truly known. There was always something bringing me down, always something to make me feel like happiness was an illusion. Then I moved here and I just...I just found it as if by accident.

"Well, there's no need to be so upset."

"These are wedding tears, not funeral tears."

Yvonne laughed softly. "Glad to hear it."

***

There was a big festive wreath on Dylan's front door when we arrived. I wondered who put it there,

197

because he didn't strike me as the decorating type. I soon discovered that Conor turned into Mr Christmas on December 24th. We knocked on the door and he threw it open, wearing the most ridiculous knitted jumper I'd ever seen.

It showed Darth Vader sipping mulled wine next to a roaring fire.

"Yvonne! Ev! You're here," he exclaimed, and I thought old Darth wasn't the only one sipping wine. I couldn't smell alcohol though, so maybe he was drunk on festive cheer.

"Hello," Yvonne greeted and he pulled her into a hug. I noticed he held on a moment longer than typical before letting go and my aunt's cheeks flushed bright red. Man, I was going to burst if they didn't figure their shit out soon.

"I'm trying to decide if your jumper is awful or inspired," I commented, and he grinned wide.

"Well, there's one in your size wrapped and under the tree, so I hope it's the latter," he shot back with a wink.

"You better be joking," I warned. "Or there'll be a Christmas morning tantrum courtesy of yours truly."

They both laughed. Conor led us inside and the house had been transformed. There were garlands twisted along the staircase, fairy lights on the bookshelves and mistletoe hanging over the doorway. There was even a giant tree in one corner of the living room donned with gold and red baubles.

"Did you do all this yourself?" I asked, impressed.

He nodded. "Yep. Christmas is my favourite time of year."

"You're such a big kid."

"Stop trying to bring me down, or I'll call you Ebenezer for the next two days."

I folded my arms and smiled. "Fine. But only because your cheerfulness is adorable."

Conor scowled playfully, just as his parents emerged from the kitchen, alongside his sister. Bethany was a few years younger than Conor, her hair in a long braid down her back. I knew them all from the Villas, and we used to say hi when we ran into each other, so they weren't complete strangers. We exchanged greetings just as Dylan's dad, Tommy, and his girlfriend, Bridget, came down the stairs.

I couldn't believe how well Tommy looked, and Bridget seemed lovely. She had short brown hair and kind eyes, and I guessed her to be in her late fifties. I was admittedly glad I lost that bet on her being a pretty young twenty-something who favoured older gentlemen.

"Evelyn! I can't believe how long it's been. And Yvonne, you look great," Tommy said as he came and gave us both hugs.

I felt a little emotional just to see him, because he was clearly in a much better place now. Life away from the Villas had been good for him, and it wasn't so much the setting as it was the memories. I couldn't imagine how hard it must be to move on when you still lived in the same flat you shared with your dead wife. It had certainly been hell for me to live in a building where my best friend's memory was so engrained.

Maybe that's why I felt lighter here in New York, where everything was new and there weren't reminders constantly bringing me down.

"This is my friend, Bridget," Tommy went on. "She's a chef."

"It's lovely to meet you," I replied and shook her hand. "You aren't by any chance cooking the turkey for tomorrow? I'm dubious about letting Conor and Dylan loose in the kitchen."

"Hey! I'm a great cook," Conor protested, overhearing me where he stood chatting with his parents.

"Yeah, yeah, I'll believe it when I see it," I teased.

"Dylan's actually doing most of the cooking," Bridget replied. "I've given him a little guidance, but other than that I'm off duty."

Speak of the devil, Dylan emerged from the kitchen wearing a green and red apron. I held back all the jokes I wanted to make, since we were in company and I knew I should behave. There was flour on the apron and I wondered what he'd been making.

His eyes landed on me first, his smile tender, and I remembered all the things he'd said to me in the car.

I might create them, but they're all you.

Warmth suffused my body as he came and greeted us. "I see everybody's met."

"Yes, and we hear you've taken on the task of preparing the food," Yvonne said. "How's it going?"

"So far so good. I just finished the mince pies."

Was it weird that I was aroused by the idea of him in the kitchen, cooking up a storm?

"Anyone for Baileys?" Conor asked and was met with a round of yeses.

"Let me show you both where you'll be staying," Dylan said, eyes on me. He pulled off the apron then led Yvonne and I upstairs. It really was a wonderful house. If Dylan ever decided to settle down, he should seriously consider buying the place.

Our room was on the second floor. It had a king-sized bed and a pretty antique vanity. I could just imagine some turn of the century lady sitting down to powder her cheeks.

"Wow, this is great," I said and dropped my bag by the foot of the bed.

"The room is gorgeous," Yvonne added.

"I'm just at the end of the hall," said Dylan, like I needed reminding. Maybe he thought I'd sneak down there in the middle of the night. With the way I was feeling about him lately, it was a definite possibility. "And the bathroom's just over here," he went on, crossing the hallway to open the door to a nice-sized bathroom.

"Yeah, we remember," I said, unsure why he was giving us the grand tour. We'd been up here before, though admittedly it was a while ago. Maybe he was just nervous. After our emotional heart to heart, I knew I was experiencing all kinds of intense feelings.

"Dad and Bridget are on the third floor, and Conor's parents and Bethany are staying on the basement level."

"You should've put us down there," I chided. "We were the last-minute invite, after all."

Dylan shook his head. "You haven't seen the basement. It's a separate little apartment with a door that leads outside. They're staying until the 28th, so we thought it best they had their own space."

Oh well, that made me feel a little better.

"Bridget seems nice," I went on, curious about what he thought.

Dylan nodded. "She's great. I like her. I was so worried she might be trying to use Dad for money or something, but she's actually really lovely."

I eyed him, dubious. "Because *that's* the only reason anyone would be interested in your dad. You of all people should know he's a catch."

He narrowed his gaze, about to say something when he shook his head. "Nope, I'm not rising to it. You're trying to rile me, I can tell."

I smirked. "He's in very good shape for his age. Isn't he, Yvonne?"

"Oh yeah, a real silver fox," she added, joining in.

Dylan put his hands in the air. "Still not rising to it. You both take your time getting settled. I'll see you downstairs." His eyes met mine briefly before he closed the door behind him.

Yvonne placed her bag up on the bed and pulled out a cardigan. She shook her head, smiling to herself. "You two."

I shot her a look. "What?"

She sighed then levelled me with a fond expression. "He loves you very much, Ev."

202

I looked away and busied myself looking around the room. Most of the drawers were empty, as was the wardrobe. When I didn't respond she continued, "And you love him."

I exhaled in exasperation. "Where are you going with this?"

"Just stating some facts. I'm not sure why you're both dancing around one another when it's obvious you should be together."

Pot meet kettle.

I didn't bother saying anything about her and Conor, because I'd already tried. She needed figure it out for herself. She pulled on her cardigan and went downstairs. I sat on the mattress, stomach turning over with butterflies as I thought about what she said. She was right about me loving Dylan, and I was certain he loved me back. What else could he have meant by telling me all his perfumes were inspired by me?

And why would he stare so deeply into my eyes and say he didn't want to be with anyone else?

Sixteen

When I finally went downstairs, there was a glass of Baileys waiting for me. I sat on the couch between Yvonne and Bethany, chatting for a while with Bethany about how she was studying nursing at college. I'd had to attend a few courses before I became Gran's primary carer, so I could relate to a lot of the things she was learning about.

Dylan was mostly in the kitchen working on dinner. At one point he emerged, still wearing that ridiculously Christmassy apron. Our eyes met, and he walked towards me. He slid his fingers through mine and pulled me up from the couch.

"I need an extra pair of hands," was all he said before he dragged me into the kitchen.

There was a cut of beef roasting in the oven, and gravy simmering in a pot on the stove.

"So, the perfumer has turned his hand to cooking," I commented.

He gave me an indulgent smile as he came and gripped my shoulders. His hands were firm, their heat sinking into my skin and warming my insides. He set me in front of a pile of potatoes and handed me a knife. When he stood behind me, I felt his chest press into my shoulders. He lowered his mouth to my ear and instructed. "Peel these."

He might as well have said, "Take off your clothes," for the way his words simmered through me, making every hair on my body stand on end.

I nodded and quietly set to work, still thinking about what Yvonne said. I wondered and I hoped. Dylan moved about the kitchen with effortless flow. You'd swear he'd been cooking all his life. But I guess in a way he had been. Designing perfumes was exactly like creating a recipe. You needed to find just the right ingredients. Figure out the exact method of combining them to achieve the desired result.

"Seems like you're not too bad a chef," I said, halfway through my peeling.

Dylan stood by the stove, alternating between stirring the gravy and checking on the roast beef. I admired the way his shirt sleeves were rolled up, revealing toned forearms.

"Have you forgotten the bruschetta I made you?"

"Right, yes, the best bruschetta in all of New York."

He smirked. "Not quite, but it's definitely up there."

I gave a soft laugh. "And what are we having for dessert?"

"Ah, now that's a surprise."

I carried the peelings to discard in the bin, while Dylan grabbed the potatoes and washed them under the tap, then threw them in a pot of boiling water. "The key to great mash is to use butter *and* milk. I also like to toss in a small teaspoon of wholegrain mustard."

"Interesting choice," I murmured just as his hand slid gently along the back of my neck. He swept my hair over one shoulder and lowered his mouth to my nape. I gasped at the contact of his soft lips on my skin, gripping the edge of the countertop.

"I've been dying to do that since you arrived," he whispered, then dragged his mouth across to my earlobe. I stifled the urge to moan, every part of me on a knife's edge already.

"Erhmmm," I murmured back, incoherent. It was so hard to concentrate on words with his lips caressing, teeth nipping.

His hand moved to circle my waist. I closed my eyes and savoured his heat. He rested his head on my shoulder and wrapped his arms around my middle. I turned my face into his and nuzzled his chin.

His mouth fell open and his breath hit my skin. It was way too hot in here and it wasn't even from the oven. Dylan held me close and neither of us moved. We stayed like that for a long while, until the potatoes started to boil over. Dylan hurried to lower the heat, while I walked to the other side of the kitchen and stared out the window.

Dylan came and stood next to me, not speaking. The windowpane was frosted on the outside from the winter chill. Our shoulders brushed when he reached down and took my hand. And then, as if by some miracle, it started to snow.

We watched the falling white flecks for a minute before an exclamation of excitement rang out from the living room. Dylan smiled down at me.

"It's snowing!" Conor announced when he burst into the kitchen. "Come on, you two. We're all going outside."

"Wait and see if it sticks first," Dylan said.

"No way. I'm going out," Conor argued before hurrying back into the living room.

I chuckled. "He really is a big kid this time of year."

"The holiday season does something funny to his brain," Dylan agreed.

In the end, the snow became so heavy that we all couldn't resist going outside. I wrapped up well and what was supposed to be a pleasant wander around the neighbourhood turned into a full-on snowball fight. It was Yvonne, Bethany and me against Dylan and Conor. Girls against boys. The 'grown-ups' were wise enough to sit it out.

I wasn't sure who won in the end, but I had snow stuck in places it had no business being stuck, courtesy of Dylan shoving snow down the back of my coat. I rewarded him by smashing some against his cheek and he gasped at the cold.

When we went inside, I savoured the warmth of the central heating and changed into some comfy leggings and a hoodie. I knew it wasn't exactly dinner attire, but I decided to choose comfort over fashion.

As expected, Dylan's food was delicious, and dessert turned out to be sherry trifle. I was pretty sure it came from a packet, since I couldn't fathom how he would have time to prepare everything from scratch.

After dinner we all gathered in the living room to watch a movie. Conor delegated himself to decide what we watched, and I couldn't help smiling when he announced his choice was *When Harry Met Sally*.

He glanced briefly at Yvonne, who appeared touched by the gesture, her cheeks flushed. I was pretty sure she hadn't watched the movie in years. I guess she didn't have to anymore. She was living the life she aspired to, but she didn't have anyone to share it with.

Sure, she had me, but a niece wasn't the same as a lover, someone you could share everything with.

Once the lights were dimmed, Dylan slid in next to me on the couch. It had been a long day and I was exhausted. I couldn't help resting my head on his shoulder as I settled into the movie. At one point, he threw his arm around me and pulled me closer so that the side of my body was flush with his. I was relaxed and peaceful, and I could've fallen asleep right there if it weren't for how his fingers stroked my hip.

The baggy hoodie I wore allowed him to slip his hand underneath and caress my skin. I had a lump in my throat and my belly was tight with need he turned me on so much. When the film ended, and everyone started making their way to their bedrooms, all I wanted to do was take Dylan's hand and lead him upstairs.

But of course, I didn't. Maybe if it was just the two of us, I'd have taken the plunge, but definitely not with a house full of people to witness my slutty behaviour. Okay, so it was hardly slutty, but still. I was too embarrassed to do something so forward. Besides, what if I did and then Dylan was all, *Ev, this isn't the time . . .*

I'd be mortified.

In our room, Yvonne and I changed into our PJs and climbed into bed. I wondered what she thought about Conor's movie choice, but decided not to pry. There was no sense meddling when I was sure they'd find their way to one another eventually.

At least, I hoped.

I lay in bed, staring at the ceiling, unable to sleep. I just couldn't stop thinking about Dylan, couldn't get the memory of his mouth on my neck out of my head. I tried everything, from counting sheep to thinking of the mundane and reassuringly attractive faces of *The Vampire Diaries* cast. Usually, that method helped me nod off, because if everyone in your universe, even the supposedly plain people, was that good-looking, the world would be a pretty worry-free place.

But no, even my failsafe wasn't working tonight.

Driven by pure frustration, I got out of bed and crept to my door. I took a deep breath, twisted the handle and stepped outside, only to find Tommy coming up the stairs. He was wearing a housecoat and held a cup of herbal tea.

Man, bumping into the parent of the person whose bedroom you were trying to sneak into for sexy times was the worst.

The *worst*.

Tommy smiled and gestured to the tea. "Bridget couldn't sleep. It's the jet lag. I thought some camomile might help."

"Oh, good idea. It took me a little while to get used to the time difference when I first moved over as well," I said and awkwardly folded my arms.

Before Tommy could say anything else, Dylan's bedroom door opened. He wore boxer shorts and a grey

T-shirt. I wondered if we'd woken him up, or if he'd been having just as much of a hard time sleeping as me. I was momentarily distracted by his scruffy bed head and bare, muscular legs when our eyes met. God, he was sexy, especially when he took in the scene and came to the most obvious conclusion. The tiniest, almost imperceptible smirk graced his lips.

Kill me. Kill me now.

He looked from me to his dad.

"Everything okay?"

"I was just taking some tea to Bridget," Tommy replied.

"And I needed to use the bathroom," I added then quickly hurried across the hall. I could hear Dylan and his dad talking while I turned on the tap and pretended to pee. They were still out there when I emerged, discussing a plan to drive to the Catskills on Wednesday for some sightseeing.

I nodded to both of them, not meeting Dylan's gaze, then shuffled back into my room.

Well, that had been a disaster.

The embarrassment seemed to kill any previous sexual desire, because I fell asleep soon after. The next morning, I didn't wake until ten. I figured everyone else was awake because Yvonne's bed was empty, and I could hear voices downstairs. I pulled my dark blue dress and glittery holiday tights out of my bag, then went to take a shower. I knew we'd just be hanging out in the house all day, but I still wanted to make an effort.

When I went downstairs, Yvonne, Dylan and Conor were in the kitchen drinking coffee. Dylan's attention fell on me, a smile in his eyes when he saw my outfit. He came forward and dipped to press a kiss on my cheek. "Merry Christmas, Ev. You look beautiful," he murmured then returned to his place by the stove.

"Are you making pancakes?"

"Yep. You want some?"

"Sure. But just one. I want to save space for dinner."

"Ev's and my Christmas tradition is to eat nothing at all until dinner time, then we gorge," Yvonne said, lifting her coffee mug for a sip.

"I like your style." Conor chuckled.

"Where's everyone else?" I asked.

"Gone out for a walk," Conor answered. "Dad likes how quiet it is on Christmas morning, the streets are always empty."

"Well, I favour not leaving the house until the twenty-sixth. You're all lucky I made the effort to get dressed," I joked and went to grab some coffee. Dylan had one of those fancy machines, and I had trouble figuring out how to use it. Yvonne and Conor chatted when he came up behind me and took the capsule from my hands.

"Like this," he said, voice low. He slotted the capsule in and pushed down the lever. I had no clue why that was sexy. It just was.

"Thanks."

"So," he continued, still hushed. "What was all that about last night?"

My pulse quickened. "Last night?"

"Out in the hallway with Dad. You looked like a rabbit caught in the headlights." There was a hint of amusement in his tone.

"I needed to use the bathroom, and I wasn't wearing a bra. Kind of embarrassing that I bumped into your dad on the way there."

"Right. Because I could've sworn you were trying to sneak into my room."

Oh, he just loved this. I shook my head. "Nope. Just a middle-of-the-night call of nature I'm afraid."

There was affection in his laugh, then his voice turned husky. "Well, if you happen to find yourself wandering the hallways again tonight, just know my door is always open."

I shivered and grabbed my coffee, then went to join the others at the table. The devilish look in Dylan's eyes would be my undoing.

The next few hours passed in a lazy fashion. I helped Dylan prepare the food, same as yesterday. And just like yesterday he drove me to the height of distraction with his little flirtations and subtle touches.

Just before dinner, my phone pinged. I casually pulled it out to check and saw a message from Mam.

Merry Christmas, Evelyn. Xxx

She sent the same text each year, and each year I didn't respond. It was petty and maybe a little selfish, I knew, but it wasn't as selfish as abandoning your own daughter when she was just fourteen years old. For some reason though, this year I felt different. We were never going to be close, but maybe I didn't need to punish her anymore. I was finding happiness in my life now, and perhaps sending Mam a simple response would help her find happiness in hers. I typed out a simple, yet meaningful reply.

Merry Christmas, Mam.

After we finished eating, we exchanged gifts. Yvonne had gotten me a red leather Guess handbag, which I just adored, and she loved her Gucci perfume set. I bought Conor a tie and Dylan a set of engraved cufflinks. I was nervous when he opened the box, hoping he liked them. It was just so hard to think of a gift. I mean, what do you buy the man who has everything?

His eyes crinkled at the edges when he saw them. We sat next to each other and I bit my lip. "Do you like them?"

He reached out and clasped my neck, surprising me when he pulled my mouth to his for quick, chaste kiss. "I love them. Thank you," he whispered.

After that I sat back and watched as everybody opened their presents, filled with a sense of belonging. It was the first time in a long time that I'd felt at peace. Like my life was going somewhere good.

Quietly, while everyone else was distracted, Dylan took my hand and led me out into the study across the hall. He closed the door and went to grab something from a drawer by the desk.

He came back with a small wrapped box and held it out to me. I took it and sat on the leather armchair in the corner. Something about this gift felt important. Dylan's eyes were full of anticipation as he watched me pull away the wrapping. Inside was a little black velvet box. I opened it up and found a pretty white gold necklace. The pendant was a circle of glass, and pressed inside the glass was a tiny dried jasmine flower.

"It beautiful," I breathed, hands shaking as I tried to undo the clasp.

Dylan knelt before me and took it from my hands. Carefully, he unclasped the latch and brought it around my neck.

"I kept this flower from when were teenagers," he said and my breath caught. I thought it was just an ordinary jasmine flower, chosen perhaps because they used to be my favourite, but it wasn't. It was special.

"Seriously?" I asked, peering down in awe. The glass pendent rested in the centre of my chest, its cool surface grazing my skin.

"I took it from the ones I picked to make my perfume when we were at school, then I put it inside some crepe paper for safekeeping. I had the pendant made at a jewellery store here in New York."

Tears sprung in my eyes. The gift was just so thoughtful, and I couldn't believe he'd kept this one flower all this time. It obviously meant something to him. And now he was giving it to me.

"I don't know what to say."

I only realised I was crying when Dylan reached out to wipe a tear from my cheek. "You don't have to say anything. Your reaction is all I need."

I studied the pendant again, taking it in my fingers and turning it over. I hadn't even noticed the engraving on the back. It read, *For Evelyn, my one true love, my muse. Yours always, Dylan.*

I inhaled sharply, unable to stop the onslaught of tears now. They ran freely down my face. Dylan made soothing noises.

"Don't cry. I gave you this to make you happy," he said, taking my face in his hands.

I blinked away some of the tears and looked at him. "I am happy. It's just . . . you're so perfect. I don't deserve you."

He gave a tender laugh. "First of all, that's not true. And second of all, that's too bad, because I'm irrevocably, hopelessly in love with you."

Before I could even digest his statement, he caught my lips in a deep, passionate kiss. He kissed me like it had to last him a lifetime. He kissed me like I was oxygen and he was gasping for breath.

I shifted forward, opening my legs so he could settle between my thighs, then wrapped my arms around his neck. He groaned, lost to our kiss, and pushed me back into the chair. He pulled my legs around his hips and held himself above me.

I moaned when I felt him harden, his thick erection pressing between my legs. He lowered his mouth to my neck, kissing my sensitive skin before he grazed his lips over the tops of my breasts. I sighed in pleasure and a base needfulness came over me. It had been weeks since I'd had him like this, and I couldn't get enough. I needed all of him, needed to touch him everywhere and have him touch me.

He hissed sharply when I reached for his belt buckle. "Careful, Ev."

"I need you," I breathed, nibbling on his lips as I stared into his eyes. "I love you, and I need you, Dylan. I feel like I've needed you forever."

His gaze burned hot. I swore the dark blue of his irises flashed black for a second when I said those words. "You love me?" he whispered.

"Yes," I answered. "I love you, Dylan O'Dea. I always have."

There was no stopping him then. He lifted my dress over my head, pulled down my tights and did away with my bra. I was left in nothing but my knickers, and he was still fully dressed. I glanced briefly at the unlocked door, hoping nobody decided to come find us. If they did, well, they were in for quite a shock.

I reached again for his buckle and this time he let me. A moment later his pants were pushed down over his hips and his cock was free. I pulled my knickers off and guided him into me. We both gasped at the sensation of being skin to skin. When he moved his hips, I moaned and bit down on his shoulder to keep quiet.

He caught my mouth and slid his tongue along mine, at the same time as he thrust inside me deeply. His eyes were open while he kissed me, taking in my every reaction. I grew so, so wet and his masculine sounds enveloped the room. He pulled away and gently clasped his hand around my neck. It was a possessive move, and every part of me pulsated with pleasure.

He drove us to dizzying heights, and when he saw on I was on the edge, he reached down between our bodies and brought me to orgasm with his fingers. I came while he was still inside me. He immediately bent and kissed my breasts, sucking one nipple into his mouth and then the other. He lapped at me until I was ready to come all over again.

A deep, raspy groan escaped him, and I knew he was almost there. I made sure I was looking deep into his eyes when he came with a shuddering expletive. He pulled out and pressed his lips to my mouth, my jaw and neck. He peppered my entire body with kisses until there wasn't an inch left untouched.

Dylan folded me in his arms, draped his shirt over our naked bodies and held me until we both fell asleep. I woke a little while later, warm from his arms around me but still chilly in the cold study. Dylan stirred, palming my breast and dipping his mouth to nibble on my ear.

"Let's go upstairs."

I batted his hand away. "We can't. Everybody's probably wondering where we've been."

"Let them wonder. Your mine now."

I let those words sink in. *You're mine now.*

It was true. I was his, and he was mine. When he started kissing me again, I knew it was time to get dressed, otherwise we were in danger of spending the rest of the evening in here, and probably the night, too. *Only a small portion of my brain insisted that wasn't a good idea.*

I swiped his hand away when he playfully pinched my hip, while I tried to put my clothes back on. I finally managed to get dressed and took a peek at myself in the small mirror on the wall, making sure I didn't look too dishevelled.

Dylan took my hand in his and I tried to ignore those pesky butterflies he always managed to solicit. I'd be ninety and still feeling belly flutters when he looked at me.

He led me back out into the living room, where Yvonne and Conor sat on the couch watching TV. They sat just a little distance apart and it made me wonder if maybe they'd grown closer over the last day and a half. There was something between them now, something new, but I couldn't quiet put my finger on it.

Tommy was napping on the armchair, while Bridget and Bethany played a game of Scrabble. I thought Conor's parents must've gone downstairs for a rest.

Conor glanced from me to Dylan and then to our clasped hands. He let out a loud, "Well, it's about time." And we both laughed at his enthusiasm. Yvonne smiled in that fond way she did, coming to give me a small hug.

"I'm so happy for you," she whispered in my ear, and it meant a lot to hear her say that. She was the only family I had left worth caring about.

We spent the rest of the evening playing board games, drinking wine and eating mince pies. When it was time for bed, I didn't give a single protest as Dylan led me to his room, laid me down, and made love to me until my body ached in the most wonderful way.

Best. Christmas. Ever.

Seventeen

"Marry me."

"Shut up."

"Ev, I'm being serious."

"No, you're not."

Dylan flipped us so he was on top, the sheets tangled between us. It was early morning, the day after Christmas, and we'd hardly gotten a wink of sleep. I was fairly sure we woke half the house during the night, in spite of our efforts to stay quiet.

"You're overtired and not thinking clearly. Give it a few hours," I said, pulse thrumming.

On the inside, I felt manic, because there was a small part of me—okay, a *big* part—that wanted him to be serious. I was head over heels in love with him and his proposal made me feel a little crazy.

Like I might do something spontaneous.

Like actually say yes.

He looked deep into my eyes, cupped my cheeks and spoke with a quiet passion that sent my nerve endings tingling.

"I've spent so many years without you. I missed you every single day. I don't want to spend a single second longer without you. Please, Ev, be my wife."

My throat ran dry as I swallowed, emotion catching right in my epiglottis. "Okay," I whispered.

He stared at me like he couldn't believe he heard me right. "Okay?"

I smiled so wide my face hurt. "Okay, Dylan. Yes, I'll marry you."

"Yes? Did you just say yes?" He looked like he didn't know what to do with himself. I nodded and smiled so wide my face hurt. "I'm going to make you the happiest woman in the world," he declared. "I promise."

"You better," I said, still smiling as I pulled his mouth to mine for a kiss.

The next thing I knew he was pulling me out of bed. "Now let's go buy you a dress."

"I have lots of time to find a wedding dress, Dylan—"

"Not if we get married today, you don't."

I grabbed him by the shoulder. "Hold up. Today?"

"Yes. We can go to City Hall and—"

"Dylan, we're not getting married today. It's the day after Christmas. They're probably not even open. Plus, I'm pretty sure you can't get a marriage licence that quickly so . . ." I paused, saddened by the disappointment in his eyes. He really wanted to do this. *Did I?* Was it too soon or had we spent months preparing for this moment? Or was that years? He had become my best friend and when I thought about it, I didn't want to spend another day without him either. Even before last night, I'd felt somewhat bereft as I'd lain in bed night after night. And that was when it clicked, when I realised I wanted to marry him today, too.

"We'll figure it out," he said. "Come on. It'll be spontaneous and wonderful and romantic. Our family is already here surrounding us. Marry me today, Ev. You'll break my heart if you say no."

I let out a long breath, but something deep inside told me this was the right decision. It was true when Dylan said we'd lost too many years, and I wasn't willing to lose another second.

"All right," I said and smiled. "Let's go buy a wedding dress."

***

My dress wasn't white, but pale pink. We found it in a small independent boutique not far from Dylan's house and I fell in love. I knew as soon as I saw it that it was the one. It was sleeveless, with a sweetheart neckline—perfect for the necklace Dylan gave me— and calf-length skirt. I adored its uniqueness and how it wasn't your typical white gown.

We didn't have time to buy rings, so instead improvised with one Gran left me in her will, and another Yvonne had at the apartment that supposedly belonged to Granddad. He died before I was born, so I had no memories of him. I only knew what he looked like from old photographs.

Dylan promised we'd go shopping for proper rings as soon as we got the chance. Yvonne thought we were being rash and impulsive, but the romantic in her couldn't help getting caught in the whirlwind. Dylan's dad welled up when we told him the news, and he was just happy he'd be there to see the ceremony.

"I always hoped you two would find each other again," he said and wiped a tear from under his eye.

Our wedding party consisted of Yvonne, Conor, Conor's parents, Bethany, Tommy and Bridget. I did my own hair and make-up, and Yvonne loaned me her nude Louboutin's to wear with my dress.

"I promise not to scuff them," I said when she handed them over. She was looking a little misty eyed when she took in the sight of me all gussied up.

"No, keep them. Consider them a wedding gift."

"But, Yvonne, I couldn't possibly—"

She held up a hand. "Don't bother protesting. They're yours now."

I decided to give her the honour of being our official witness. After we applied for our marriage licence, we hustled across the street from City Hall to get a waiver from the judge. This was so we didn't have to wait twenty-fours before getting married.

The ceremony took less than two minutes.

The whole thing was insane, but I had no regrets. I was on cloud nine, no intention of ever coming back down. It was moments like these that I really felt like Sam was watching, grumping about not being able to take part in the excitement and spontaneity.

"Evelyn O'Dea, I like the sound of that," Dylan purred as we slow-danced in some random bar on the lower east side.

Yvonne and Conor were cosying it up at a table, deep in conversation, while everyone else enjoyed bar food and drinks. It was completely unconventional and that's why it felt so perfect.

"Me, too," I said, catching his lips in a quick kiss.

"If someone told me I'd be married to you before the year was through, I never would've believed them."

"You've got to believe in the power of the universe," I said. "It pulled us back together." Damn, I was on such a high I almost sounded like my teenage self.

He ran a hand down my hair and gazed at me with such love. "Better thank the universe then."

"Yep," I whispered just as a loud *pop* sounded from behind us. Conor and Yvonne had ordered several bottles of champagne. Dylan chuckled and took my hand to lead me over. My aunt was in fine form, pouring glasses for everyone.

"Here you go, Ev," she said and handed one to me. "Happy wedding day."

"To Dylan and Evelyn. May they have many years of happiness and romantic bliss ahead of them," Conor declared, lifting his glass.

"Here, here," everyone agreed and we all took a drink.

I didn't remember much after that, only that a lot of alcohol was consumed, and much dancing and merriment was had. The next morning, I woke in Dylan's bed, completely naked, our bodies entwined.

We called in sick to work.

We made love all day and through the next night.

We ordered pizza. Lots of pizza. It was the best honeymoon a girl could ask for.

When the following morning arrived, we sadly said goodbye to our mini-vacation.

I lay on top of Dylan, drawing circles on his chest with my finger. "I still can't believe we just decided to get hitched like a pair of whack jobs."

"Not like pair of whack jobs, like a pair of geniuses," he corrected.

My smile transformed into a grin. "Oh, is that what we are?"

"Yes," he said and rolled me over. "Now go get dressed. We have rings to shop for."

Less than an hour later, I stood in the middle of a jewellery shop on Fifth Avenue, an array of diamonds before me. It was surreal to say the least.

"This is weird. A lady shouldn't have to shop for her own engagement ring. And certainly not after the fact of getting married," I said, playful and trying to annoy Dylan.

The rings viewed so far had prices in the five-figure category. I was trying to finagle him down to four.

"I just wouldn't feel comfortable walking around with over ten grand on my finger," I said. "That's the sort of thing that gets your hand chopped off in the supermarket."

He gave me a funny look. "What on earth are you talking about?"

"Haven't you heard the story of the woman whose hand was chopped off while she was shopping for groceries? The guy who did it was after her engagement ring."

He stared at me, looking dubious. "And where exactly did this happen?"

"Germany, I think. Or was it South Africa?"

He arched a wry brow. "Smacks of an urban legend, Ev."

"Either way, I don't want any of these overpriced rings. They're too ostentatious."

He let out a sigh and slid his hand into mine, steering me to another glass cabinet. "Fine. What about one of these?"

I studied the collection. "Still expensive, but acceptable."

"I like this one," Dylan said, pointing out a white gold ring with a teardrop shaped diamond.

"It's very pretty," I commented. And it was. It was beautiful, all sparkly under the fluorescent lights.

"Do you like it?"

"Of course."

"Then we'll buy it," he said and waved the sales clerk over.

I grabbed his arm. "Hold up. We can't buy it just like that. We should wait a few days. Shop around to see if there's a better deal somewhere else—"

"Ev, I'm buying it, so build a bridge."

I poked him in the side. "*You* build a bridge."

The sales clerk arrived. "How may I help you, sir?"

"I'd like to buy this ring."

"Very well, sir."

And that was how I found myself walking around with a brand-new diamond on my finger. It felt bizarre. When Dylan left to go to work, I decided it was time I went to the apartment to pack. During our 'honeymoon', Dylan convinced me to move in with him. Albeit, it didn't take too much convincing. Now that we were married, why would I have even considered spending a single night alone?

I walked into the apartment, making plans for how I was going to pack and move all my stuff, and came face to face with Conor stepping out of the bathroom.

I repeat, Conor Abrahams just stepped out of *my* bathroom. Steam billowed behind him. He wore a towel and nothing else, stopping short as soon as he saw me.

And it suddenly dawned on me. I hadn't seen him since his family left.

He'd been here.

With Yvonne.

Oh. My. God.

A sense of pure delight filled me. My aunt was going to get some serious ribbing for this. And I had so many questions. Like, how had this come about? Did it happen on the night of the wedding, or afterwards, while Dylan and I were wrapped in our own little sex bubble?

"Conor, what time are you—" Yvonne's voice trailed off when she saw me standing there.

"Ev," she exclaimed. It was almost a shriek. "I thought you'd be with Dylan."

"He had to go to work."

"As do I," Conor cut in. "I'll just, uh, go get dressed."

He disappeared inside Yvonne's bedroom, while I folded my arms and shot my aunt a smug look. "Well," I chirped.

She pursed her lips. "Well, what?"

I shook my head. "Just, well."

Walking past her, I went to hang my things. I could practically feel her embarrassment and anxiety simmering to a high heat. "Listen, Ev—"

"No need to explain, Yvonne. If I were you, I'd have hit that on the first night."

"*Evelyn.*"

I smirked. "What? It's true. You go, girlfriend."

"Ugh. You're so pleased with yourself right now," she huffed.

I cocked a brow. "Aren't you?"

"No, I'm not. If my mother were alive, I shudder to think what she'd say."

"If Gran were alive, she'd say exactly the same thing as I just did."

That got a small smile out of her and then she laughed. "Do you know what, you're probably right."

"I'm always right. Now go say goodbye to your lover and wish him a good day at work."

She let out a shaky breath. "My lover. It sounds weird."

"It does sound weird," Conor agreed when he emerged from Yvonne's bedroom. She jumped a little, realising he'd overheard. He leaned down and pressed a kiss to her lips. "Boyfriend sounds so much better."

With a pleased wink and a smirk, he hustled out the door. He didn't just look pleased though. He looked euphoric, smug . . . happy. It wasn't just that he had been infatuated with Yvonne. In his own way, he'd loved her for a very long time. So, he had every right to be feeling smug, but I thought it was happiness that shone the brightest.

228

Yvonne's gaze met mine. "Boyfriend," she repeated.

"Congratulations, you're officially a cougar," I teased, smiling wide.

She scowled playfully and grabbed a cushion from the sofa. She came at me, thumping me on the head and demanding, "I am not a cougar. Take that back."

"Okay, fine," I relented. "You're not a cougar. I take it back. You're a lion cub, a cute and adorable baby lion with no wrinkles and the most youthful appearance."

She stopped her attack and threw the cushion back on the couch, a huge grin on her face. "And don't you forget it."

After she left for work, I took a moment to reflect on our lives. We were thrown together many years ago, which could have resulted in a very different future. One less hopeful. Yvonne had been there for me through every stage of my life when I thought about it. She'd held me, laughed with me, cried with me, mourned with me, hoped with and for me. *Selflessly.* Now, with her final acceptance of Conor, it was almost as though knowing I was finally happy, had finally found *my* home with Dylan, that she had opened her heart for herself.

I wouldn't forget it. I wouldn't forget any of our moments together, because they'd made me who I was. And I could step confidently into my future because of her many years of selfless and deep love. And may there be many, many more.

Epilogue

6 months later

"You've done a wonderful job," Frank said, and I was thrilled with the praise. He'd happened by, like he often did, hands in his pockets.

When Dylan introduced us at the charity event last year, the flower farm owner had offered me a job, something of an open invitation. After a few more months bartending, I woke up one morning and decided to hell with it. I was going to take him up on his offer. I never realised how much I missed growing until I accepted the job here at Hillview. My passion for gardening was coming back little by little. With every new crop I helped harvest, I felt like I was finding my old self again.

I no longer looked on the world through a dark lens. Now I understood that everything had to die so that new things could come to life.

I'd only been working here a month and already it felt like home. Don't get me wrong. The commute was rough, almost two hours there and back. But I only worked four days a week, so at least I had three days to recuperate.

I wiped the sweat from my brow and gazed at Frank.

"How did everything go at the doctors?" I asked.

He shrugged. "Prescribed me more painkillers and anti-inflammatory pills. The usual. I'm too old to be cured." Frank suffered with chronic back pain, a result

231

of years working to build his farm. Never let it be said that gardening was easy work.

"Well, if you ever want to start some hydroponics, just say the word. You know, for the pain."

He smiled fondly. "We can get that on a prescription here, dearie."

I made a silly face. "Right. Sorry."

"Not trying to get me into drug dealing in my golden years?"

"Sounds like the plot to a good TV show."

"Eh. It's been done."

I feigned disappointment. "Dammit."

"Anyway, you're too good of a gardener to be dabbling in TV. The world of flower farming needs you."

"Feels good to be needed."

"Yeah well, if that husband of yours ever wants to move out of Manhattan, you two can come run this place for me. My old bones have had enough manual labour for one lifetime."

"Ah, and you make it sound *so* appealing." I joked, and yet, the idea spoke to my heart. I pictured myself in a few years' time, running Frank's flower farm with Dylan by my side. It was definitely possible.

He chuckled. "Right well, I'm going inside for a lie down. I'll see you next week."

"See you next week, Frank," I said and gave him a little wave.

When I was done with my shift, I cleaned up and started the journey home. Tonight was the launch of *Samuel,* and I was so excited. Even though I'd been involved in creating the scent, naturally Dylan and his marketing team had done the rest. I had faith that they'd create something wonderful. The last few weeks Dylan would randomly pepper me with questions like, *What was Sam's favourite colour? His favourite song?*

I knew he was trying to design a visual that paid tribute to him in some way, and I was eager for the big reveal. I think he wanted it to be a surprise, though, because every time I asked how things were coming along, he got all cagey and wouldn't give me any details.

When I got home, the house was empty. I showered and changed into the black silk dress I bought especially for the launch. The party was being held at the Waldorf, so I knew I had to wear something fancy.

Dylan organised for a town car to take Yvonne, Conor and me to the hotel, since he'd been there all day taking care of the last-minute arrangements. It still felt a little surreal that this was my life, but then, not at all. Wherever Dylan was, whatever his world entailed, that was where I would be. Whether we had to live in a tiny flat in Dublin, or in a historic old townhouse on New York's Lower East Side, I'd be there with him and vice versa.

"I hear congratulations are in order," came a familiar voice I hadn't heard in years.

I turned and saw a woman with short dark hair wearing a green dress. I was stunned, for one because I don't think I ever saw her wear a dress before, and two because of the gorgeous woman she'd become.

Amy threw her arms around my shoulders and pulled me into a hug. "Oh my God, it's so good to see you," I exclaimed. "What on earth are you doing here?"

"Didn't Dylan tell you? I helped with footage for the ad," she replied.

I remembered Dylan briefly telling me how Amy lived in London with her husband and two kids, and that she worked in film. It made sense given her obsession with recording everything when we were younger.

I shook my head. "No, he's actually been keeping pretty schtum about the whole thing. I think he wants it to be a surprise."

Some sort of understanding dawned on her when she replied, "Ah yes, I can understand why."

I didn't question her further, because it wasn't long before the ad would be revealed to everyone at the launch. We drank wine and chatted about her life in London, her husband and kids. When we first met, Amy and I had been chalk and cheese, but once Dylan became my boyfriend, I found a new friend in her. Even though our lives hadn't crossed for years, there was no awkwardness. We could talk comfortably just that same as we used to. And I was glad she'd left the Villas behind. Just like Dylan and Conor, she was never meant for that place. I was delighted everything had worked out so well for her.

I only caught flashes of Dylan flitting about the room, mingling with guests and charming everyone. Our eyes met once or twice, his expression promising he'd get to me soon. But then there was an announcement over the speakers, instructing everyone to gather in front of the projector screen. The lights were dimmed, and a sense of eager anticipation filled the room. My pulse thrummed as I finished my wine, set my glass on a table, and waited to see what my husband had been keeping secret from me these last few weeks.

The screen lit up and I instantly recognised the scene, even though I'd never seen the video before. It showed grainy black-and-white footage of Sam and me sitting side by side on the staircase at the Villas. My breath caught as piano music filled my ears.

When Dylan asked what was Sam's favourite song, I told him there was a certain part of Rachmaninov's piano concerto No. 2 that always made him well up. Yvonne used to have it playing while she pottered around the flat.

A little over two minutes into the piece, there was a part where Sam always clutched his chest and said it was most romantic bit of music he'd ever heard. I'd slag him about being so sloppy and sentimental, but he'd just stick his tongue out at me, not giving a care to my teasing.

Somehow, the music fit perfectly with the footage. It laced together the images of the five of us: Sam, Dylan, Conor, Amy and me. We all looked so young, so baby-faced and full of hope. Unbidden, tears filled my eyes, but I didn't care about ruining my mascara right then. I couldn't believe what Dylan had created. I'd never seen any of this footage, had always brushed off

Amy's little obsession as silliness. But now, now it was everything my heart needed to see.

The screen zoomed in on Sam's smiling face after I said something to him. I'd never forget that smile, but it still felt so good to see it again. The black and white switched to colour, the camera focusing in on each of us on the roof of the Villas. Someone grabbed Amy's camera and faced it on her. She scowled, but you could see her amusement as she snatched it back. I knew it was Sam when she held it up again and he wore a cheeky grin.

The ad ended with a simple statement scrawled across the screen.

The best memories live on forever in our hearts. Samuel*, a new fragrance from Dylan.*

I wiped at my tears, but it was no use. They just kept falling. Dylan appeared in front of me and took each of my hands in his.

"I . . . I don't know what to say," I whispered.

"You're crying," he said, taking me in.

"They're happy tears," I replied. "Dylan, that was beautiful."

He pulled me into a hug. "I hope we did him justice."

"You did that and more. That's the most thoughtful thing anyone's ever done for me."

He held me for a long moment, and then people descended, telling Dylan how much they loved the ad, how touching and unique it was, how kind he was being by donating half of the profits to charity.

I stood next to him the entire time, his hand in mine, smiling while we met person after person. For the first time in forever, I didn't think of Sam and feel sad. I thought of him and felt happy for all the good times we'd shared. The happiness and the laughter. He'd been the best friend a girl could ask for, and though he was taken too soon, I was glad to have known him.

For a brief time, his sunshine and cheerfulness, his brazenness and sass, had lit up my world.

Somehow, the short video purged all my lingering, hidden sadness, but I sensed it was cathartic for Dylan, too. For years, he'd felt guilty for Sam's death. This was his way of getting it all out, of paying tribute. His way of healing. Of understanding that his heart was pure.

I glanced at the man beside me and fell in love even deeper, because he'd flicked the switch. He'd turned on the light bulb in my mind, shown me a new way of thinking just like he did when we were teenagers.

Only this time, I didn't hate the world. I didn't see the cracks.

I saw all the beautiful, flawed and wonderful parts that held them all together.

End.

About the Author

L.H. Cosway lives in Dublin, Ireland. Her inspiration to write comes from music. Her favourite things in life include writing stories, vintage clothing, dark cabaret music, food, musical comedy, and of course, books. She thinks that imperfect people are the most interesting kind. They tell the best stories.

Find L.H. Cosway online!

www.lhcoswayauthor.com
www.twitter.com/LHCosway
www.facebook.com/LHCosway
www.instagram.com/l.h.cosway

L.H. Cosway's *HEARTS* Series

Praise for *Six of Hearts* (Book #1)

"This book was sexy. Man was it hot! Cosway writes sexual tension so that it practically sizzles off the page." - A. Meredith Walters, New York Times & USA Today Bestselling Author.

"Six of Hearts is a book that will absorb you with its electric and all-consuming atmosphere." - Lucia, Reading is my Breathing.

"There is so much "swoonage" in these pages that romance readers will want to hold this book close and not let go." - Katie, Babbling About Books.

Praise for *Hearts of Fire* (Book #2)

"This story holds so much intensity and it's just blazing hot. It created an inferno of emotions inside me." - Patrycja, Smokin' Hot Book Blog.

"I think this is my very favorite LH Cosway romance to date. Absolutely gorgeous." - Angela, Fiction Vixen.

"Okay we just fell in love. Complete and utter beautiful book love. You know the kind of love where you just don't want a book to finish. You try and make it last; you want the world to pause as you read and you

want the story to go on and on because you're not ready to let it go." - Jenny & Gitte, Totally Booked.

Praise for *King of Hearts* (Book #3)

"Addictive. Consuming. Witty. Heartbreaking. Brilliant--King of Hearts is one of my favourite reads of 2015!" - Samantha Young, New York Times, USA Today and Wall Street Journal bestselling author.

"I was looking for a superb read, and somehow I stumbled across an epic one." - Natasha is a Book Junkie.

"5+++++++ Breathtaking stars! Outstanding. Incredible. Epic. Overwhelmingly romantic and poignant. There's book love and in this case there's BOOK LOVE." - Jenny & Gitte, Totally Booked.

Praise for *Hearts of Blue* (Book #4)

"From its compelling characters, to the competent prose that holds us rapt cover to cover, this is a book I could not put down." - Natasha is a Book Junkie.

"Devoured it in one sitting. Sexy, witty, and fresh. Their love was not meant to be, their love should never *work, but Lee and Karla can't deny what burns so deep and strong in their hearts. Confidently a TRSoR recommendation and fave!"*- The Rock Stars of Romance.

"WOW!!! It's hard to find words right now, I don't think the word LOVE even makes justice or can even describe how much I adored this novel. Karla handcuffed my senses and Lee stole my heart."- Dee, Wrapped Up In Reading

Praise for *Thief of Hearts* (Book #5)

"This is easily one of our favorite romances by L.H. Cosway. We were consumed by the brilliant slow-burn and smoldering student/teacher forbidden storyline with layers of uncontainable, explosive raw emotions and genuine heart." – The Rock Stars of Romance.

"I was in love with this couple and was championing their relationship from the start." – I Love Book Love

"One of my fave reads of this year. Mind-blowing and thrilling, let this story sweep you off your feet!" – Aaly and the Books.

Books by L.H. Cosway

Contemporary Romance
Painted Faces
Killer Queen
The Nature of Cruelty
Still Life with Strings
Showmance

The Cracks Duet
A Crack in Everything (#1)
How the Light Gets in (#2)

The Hearts Series
Six of Hearts (#1)
Hearts of Fire (#2)
King of Hearts (#3)
Hearts of Blue (#4)
Thief of Hearts (#5)
Hearts on Air (#6)

The Rugby Series with Penny Reid
The Hooker & the Hermit (#1)
The Player & the Pixie (#2)
The Cad & the Co-ed (#3)

Urban Fantasy
Tegan's Blood (The Ultimate Power Series #1)
Tegan's Return (The Ultimate Power Series #2)
Tegan's Magic (The Ultimate Power Series #3)
Tegan's Power (The Ultimate Power Series #4)